Cassie grabbed Matt's chin with her hand, holding it.

'You asked me about myself,' she started, trying to ignore the warm flesh beneath her fingers. 'You know I'm a time management consultant, engaged to be married and happy with the idea of financial security.'

Her body heated at the contact and the deep promise in Matt's eyes. She dropped her hand. 'So that's it. That's where I'm at, what I'm planning and where I'm heading.'

Matt grabbed her by the shoulder and pulled her closer to him. 'You can't do that.'

Darcy Maguire wanted to grow up to be a fairy, but her wings never grew, her magic never worked and her life was no fairytale. But one thing she knew for certain was that she was going to find her soul-mate and live happily ever after. Darcy found her dark and handsome hero on a blind date, married him a year later and found that love truly is the soul of creativity.

With four children too young to play matchmaker for (yet!), Darcy satisfies the romantic in her by finding true love for her fictional characters. It was this passion for romance, and her ability to sit still every day, that led to the publication of her first novel, HER MARRIAGE SECRET. Darcy lives in Melbourne, Australia, and loves to read widely, sew and sneak off to the movies without the kids.

Darcy Maguire is a fresh, exciting new talent in Tender Romance™. Her lively, emotional stories and colourful characters make her a name to watch!

Look out for future novels by Darcy Maguire in Tender Romance™.

ALMOST MARRIED

BY
DARCY MAGUIRE

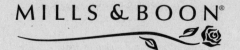

MILLS & BOON®

First published in Great Britain 2003
Harlequin Mills & Boon Limited,
Eton House, 18-24 Paradise Road, Richmond, Surrey TW9 1SR

© Debra D'Arcy 2003

ISBN 0 263 83360 7

Set in Times Roman 10½ on 12½ pt.
02-0303-42795

Printed and bound in Spain
by Litografia Rosés, S.A., Barcelona

CHAPTER ONE

CASSIE struggled to open her eyes but light streamed onto her and pain flared. What had she been drinking last night?

She scrunched her eyes shut and pulled the soft covers up, coaxing her tongue off the roof of her mouth. No way was she facing the morning.

A cough. Deep. Male.

Cassie managed a smile. It was only a week now until she married Sebastian. Intelligent, ambitious Sebastian. It'd be around seven-twenty a.m., give or take a minute or two. He'd be getting ready for work—meticulously combing down his sandy hair, picking off any specks of dust on his suit, choosing which silk tie to wear, and neatly stacking his papers into his black attaché case. She should see him out.

She opened her eyes gingerly, focussing on the pillow beside her, and the indentation in it where her fiancé would have lain. A rose appeared in the thinning blur. A perfect red rose, just starting to bloom.

The rich scent drifted to her and she smiled—it wasn't like Sebastian to be romantic. She ran a hand over the soft pillow, over the now-cool impression in it, and up to touch the delicate petals of the rose. 'Hmm, what time is it?'

'You're awake. Good.'

Cassie froze. That wasn't Sebastian's voice! It was deeper, huskier, and totally alien to her. She sat up. Her brain lurched and dizziness challenged her.

A stranger stood near the end of the bed. He looked in his early thirties, wore black trousers, and a white shirt that hugged his wide shoulders and was tucked in against a flat stomach. A swath of rusty-brown hair fell casually on his forehead and dark eyes framed a boldly handsome face. His hands were large and square—he was resting one thumb on his full lips, stifling what looked to be a smile.

'What…?' she gasped. 'Who the blazes are you?'

'Matthew Keegan. And you are?'

His casual tone rippled through her. She scanned the room. It wasn't home. It wasn't Sebastian's. The walls were neither her pastel peach nor his bold whites; it was an alien lemon colour. The furniture was modern, the window frames flush with the wall. 'I'm lost.'

'And naked.'

Cassie looked down. She was! She grabbed the sheet and yanked it to her chin, covering herself. And took another look. She *was* completely naked! Heat suffused her cheeks and her mind jerked. What was she doing without anything on? She always wore a nightie. Always. 'Where's Sebastian?' she squeaked.

He cocked an eyebrow. 'Who?'

She racked her mind for answers, for questions, but all sense was traitorously absent. 'What am I doing here?'

'I think that's obvious.' The stranger took a deep

breath and dropped his gaze to the floor. 'We had a great time.'

Cassie swallowed hard. This couldn't be happening. Not to her. She was plain. Boring even. Same job, same apartment, even the same hairdo for the last five years! Situations like this just didn't happen to people like her.

'We didn't…?' She frowned at the pillow beside her. 'I didn't…? Not with you!'

The man nodded. 'We sure did.' He turned away, straightening his shirt. 'Now, if you'll excuse me. I've got work to do.' He turned to the chair placed at the end of the bed and picked up a file.

'No wait.' Cassie held up her hand. She needed answers. This didn't make sense. She would never have…

He moved swiftly, carrying himself with a commanding air of purpose, heading for the door.

'Please wait.' She leapt up and staggered from the bed, dragging the sheet with her, trying to hold it around her, trying to cover every inch of her from him. She strained to remember last night but her brain was as mutinous as her legs. 'I…I can't remember.'

He turned and pierced her with his dark eyes, his long fingers clamping around the handle on the narrow door. 'Don't worry about it. You were great.'

Cassie's breath caught in her throat. She raised her chin slowly, glaring up at him. He had to be at least a head taller than her and he *was* handsome enough to catch her attention, *and* his cologne was enticing, but she wouldn't have done anything. Not with a stranger, especially one as arrogant as this guy.

He had the nerve to offer her a smile.

She slapped his face. Hard. 'That's not what I meant,' she bit out. 'Who the hell are you?' She pulled the sheet closer around her, her palm stinging.

'I told you, Matt Keegan.' He rubbed his cheek, her handprint blazing boldly on his flesh. 'And you are?'

She stared into his rich dark eyes. She bit her lip. 'You don't know *my name*?'

'No.' He cleared his throat. 'We were…' his attention wandered slowly down her sheet to her bare feet '…too involved in other things.'

Cassie's stomach curled and her nerves reeled. 'No.' She shook her head violently, a dry ache clinging to the back of her throat clawing for release.

He nodded, averting his eyes as he turned away from her.

She grabbed his jacket sleeve and felt his muscles clench under her touch, heard his sharp intake of breath. 'You don't understand. I'm getting married next weekend,' she blurted. And it was going to be a beautiful summer wedding with all the trimmings, all her family, all perfect. Except for this!

He avoided her eyes. 'You couldn't love him that much. You slept with me.'

Her blood fired. 'I may have woken up in your bed—'

'Naked.'

'Naked.' She stared at his chest where his top button was undone, revealing the lightest scatter of dark whorls. 'But…but that doesn't mean anything happened.'

'Doesn't it? I seem to recall several interesting things…'

She held up her hand to stop him. Her mind filled in the pieces, feeding the ache in her stomach. 'If you were anything as drunk as me—' but for the life of her she couldn't remember how she'd managed to get plastered on the few drinks she'd had. '—we'd have been hard pressed doing anything.'

'Right. If you say so.' He gave her a look, one where his eyes smiled at her while his mouth didn't. 'If that makes you feel better.'

It didn't. Cassie scowled at the man. She couldn't believe they'd done nothing, not with him looking as he did.

She needed to know how exactly this could have happened, and why. And fast. Her wedding was only five days away.

CHAPTER TWO

MATT KEEGAN strode through the doorway and slammed the door behind him. How the hell had he got mixed up in this?

He charged up the corridor. He would never have thought telling a woman she'd slept with him could be so distasteful, so jarring on his conscience. But he'd had no choice.

A man in a smart white and blue uniform intercepted him. 'Mr Keegan? They're waiting for you on the bridge.'

'On my way.' He glanced at his watch. That woman had assured him it would only be a few minutes before the stranger in his cabin would wake. It had been two hours. He couldn't have shaken her awake. He would rather have read the damned file he'd had with him twenty thousand times than wake her. What he'd done was bad enough without adding scaring her to death.

Work. Matt sucked in his breath. Focus on work. It was important, familiar, and safe. But his mind wandered.

Her hair was so black, cropped almost as short as his own. And he hadn't missed how her creamy white skin was stained with the make-up of the night before, but it was her deep green eyes that had caught him off guard—those and her breasts.

He ran a hand through his hair and lengthened his stride, pushing the stir of desire down. He shouldn't have done it. She'd looked so hurt, so concerned, so utterly lost.

Rob flashed into his mind and he felt a different, but all-too-familiar ache in his gut. He sighed. There was nothing else he could have done…

The bridge of the cruise ship was a testament to modern technology. The controls were state of the art. Matt couldn't help but smile. His company had been commissioned for decking the new cruise ship out with all the latest technology. It was one of their biggest contracts yet.

The captain turned. 'Glad you could make it. You missed the launch.'

'I know. Other commitments. How'd it go?' Matt cast a glance out of the front windows at the vast ocean in front of them, and at the bow of the huge expanse of cruise ship beneath them.

'Like clockwork. Smooth as silk.'

Matt savoured the swell of satisfaction in his chest. His team had overseen the operation and had ensured the launch was textbook. He hadn't expected anything less.

He patrolled the terminals, perusing the equipment his company had installed, reading the data on the screens over the operators' shoulders—a totally integrated operating system for the liner. He was proud of what they'd built, of *all* that they'd achieved in the last decade.

He hailed Carl. He was a burly man, more suited to ride a Harley than sit at a keyboard. 'Where's Rob?'

Carl shoved his sleeves up to his elbows, his red and black tattoo of a cobra making an appearance. 'Deck C. Security office. Got some glitch down there.'

Matt nodded. Rob would handle that, no problems. He smiled. Work was something *he* could handle, too. Far more predictable than his private life.

His mind threw up the morning's encounter again, dwelling on her. At least his part was played and he didn't have to do anything else. He could probably even forget it had ever happened, if he could push the image of her vulnerability from his mind.

He took a seat and centred his attention on the job at hand. He took a deep, calming breath. He didn't have to worry. It was over. No more lies.

Cassie leant against the door, pressing her fingers against her temples. She stared at her clothes strewn across the sitting room, lying where they must have fallen, as she'd shed them, all the way to the bed.

Breathe, just breathe. Don't panic. This may not be what it looks like. It could have been staged. It could all be a joke. Her office pals and girlfriends were always in for a laugh. She stared around the quiet room and a weight pressed down on her. This wasn't funny.

Goose-flesh rippled along her arms. Memories flooded back. Of her first crush. Of a cruel joke.

At fourteen she'd been an easy victim, wearing her heart pinned on her blazer for all to see. It hadn't been a secret that she'd liked that boy. Far from it. It had been the in-thing to discuss in the girlie huddles at recess and at lunch, whispering over who'd liked whom. She'd known she'd never had a chance, everyone had liked him and she'd been far from perfect, still carrying her baby-round cheeks and puppy-fat.

The valentine's card that had been in her locker had been crude, but the messy scrawl inside had said it all. *He'd* liked her. Her heart had fluttered, her naïve hopes rising.

He'd met her behind the portables, asked her to go steady and she'd been idiot enough to believe every word. It had been the shortest run in history. Ten minutes later she'd seen him with most of her class, laughing. She should have ignored them. But hadn't. She'd had to get the punchline of the joke served to her, in front of everyone, by *him*, because she hadn't had the sense to leave it be.

She swallowed hard, and darted a look at her bare wrist. Where in blazes was her watch?

A clock on the desk blinked the time. Ten-thirty.

Cassie looked to the ceiling. Her whole schedule was out the window! What would her nine o'clock think of her now? And her ten o'clock? Not exactly the model of punctuality and control she prided herself and her staff to be. Her time-management consultancy would be a láughing-stock if her staff didn't rise to the occasion.

The room swayed.

She flung out her arms. Either she was still drunk or there was a movement to the room, a vibration to the floor.

The room was compact. She'd guess a motel or a caravan unit of some sort by the panelled look of the walls, the economy of space, the frugal use of furniture and the total lack of any personal touches.

The window was large and sealed. Cassie pressed her fingers against the glass. The blue sky stretched upwards and water tossed below. She stared out to sea.

She was still on the ship!

She steadied herself, placing both her palms on the cool surface of the glass. She longed to take a gulp of fresh air to clear her head, to help her make sense of this.

There was no land in sight.

Where the blazes was she going?

She stood motionless in the middle of the room, her mind grappling to make sense of how this could possibly have happened to her.

Images of her hen-night were clear and strong in her mind. It had been a lovely surprise for her last night. She hadn't expected all her friends and workmates, just an intimate dinner on the liner with her very own up-and-coming politician. Sebastian must have wrangled the favour through his connections. Just one evening. Not a blinking cruise!

There'd been laughing, music and the nicest presents. She looked around the cabin. Had her friend, Eva, taken the gifts with her? If she had, then why had she left her, the bride-to-be, behind?

Cassie kneaded her hands together. She needed her daily planner. Her entire life was in it. She took a long, slow breath. It was Monday. It was too late to do anything about today's appointments, but she needed to know what else she was missing. She needed to hold her planner, press it closely to her chest, needed to figure out whether she'd make it to her own wedding!

She turned and stepped over to the pile of black fabric near the door—her pleated trousers. She picked them up and clutched them tightly. Her cream blouse lay stretched across the floor as though the need to get to the bed had outweighed any decorum or tidiness. She cringed and picked it up. Her bra was draped over the arm of the chair in the corner, and her pants hidden in the covers of the bed. She swallowed hard. *This was no prank.*

This wasn't fair. Cassie stamped her foot. Just when she'd figured her life was all going to work out perfectly some idiot came along and wrecked it all.

Her watch lay on the floor beside the bedside table. Cassie stroked the face and ran her hand over the gold band, watching the seconds pass slowly. Time was something she *could* rely on.

Cassie placed her watch reverently over the pale band of skin on her wrist, feeling better for the contact, for the security—at least she knew the time.

The room didn't hold any more of her belongings and there was still no sign of her handbag. She chewed her lower lip. There was the chance that she'd been robbed while she'd been drunk, but how had she ended up here, like this, with *that* man?

She stalked to the *en suite* bathroom and stared at her wide-eyed reflection. Sebastian would be worried about her. He liked to know where she was and who she was with. She'd have to get a message to him, call him if she could—he'd work this out for her.

She put her finger in her mouth, resting the nail on her teeth. What would Sebastian say when he found out? All her plans. All ruined now. All because of that man.

There was no doubt in her mind that Matt Keegan was attractive and unscrupulous enough to take any woman, no matter what. Drunk or not. Engaged or not. And that left her here, like this, stranded.

Cassie donned her clothes and stabbed her feet into her heels. Sebastian didn't need to find out. No one knew who she was on this ship… Hell, *she* didn't even know where she was, except on an ocean heading away from Australia.

Her heart sank to her toes. What had happened?

She sat down heavily on the edge of the bed. Why couldn't her life be simple?

Cassie straightened. She'd managed through everything life had thrown her way so far. This needn't be any different.

She wasn't going to take this lying down. She glanced behind her to the rumpled bed and winced.

She was going to find out exactly what had happened between her and Matt Keegan—drum home to him what an inconsiderate jerk he was, then go home and get married. End of story.

CHAPTER THREE

'MR KEEGAN.' An officer nudged him on the shoulder.

Matt raised a hand. He didn't need any interruptions. He'd monitored the system for the last two hours, without a hiccup, and the diagnostic was almost done. Just a few more minutes…

He figured he had to be one of the luckiest men alive to have had the breaks he'd had. He'd won a scholarship at Bond University, then landed a job with Thomas Boyton, an enterprising businessman who looked to the future. Thomas had backed him with opening a specialised branch of computronics making all Matt's dreams come true. His team had to be the best in Australia. Everything was going his way.

The man beside him cleared his throat. 'Mr Keegan. There's a woman asking for you.'

Matt watched the numbers roll past on the screen. 'A what?'

'A woman.' The young man shuffled his feet. 'You know—' he lowered his voice '—the opposite gender.'

His mind grappled for the significance. Who the hell would be interrupting him now? Work was work, damn it. Matt glanced up from the terminal.

She stood in the doorway. She'd showered. And dressed. Trousers covered her long legs, and a blouse hid her full breasts. Her jet-black hair was combed down, parted on her right side, sweeping across her forehead. Her green eyes stabbed him, hitting him deep in his chest.

He swallowed hard. 'Fine. Tell her to wait. I'll be out shortly.' He dismissed the officer and ducked his head back down, fighting off his clawing guilt.

He tried to concentrate on the data streaming onto the screen, to focus on work…he had to think, to analyse. If these figures came up the way the practice-run anticipated, this trip could very easily be seen as a well-deserved break, rather than work… In a perfect world, anyway. Matt knew work and computers well enough to know plans went awry very easily.

'Sir?'

'What?' Matt snapped. He punched a key and glared at the young officer, daring him to divulge any more news he didn't want to hear.

The officer shifted awkwardly. 'She's quite insistent. She refuses to leave the doorway.'

'So? Let her stand there.' He clenched his fist, refusing to look at the door again. The deal was for five minutes of dialogue, that was it. He swallowed hard. He couldn't be expected to keep on with the charade.

'She's blocking traffic, sir.'

Damn it. He'd known it was going to be harder than they'd said. Nothing was simple, especially when you threw a woman into the mix. He saved the data, stabbing the keys. 'Carl, can you print this out?' he barked.

Carl glanced up, raising an eyebrow, obviously aware of the situation standing attractively at the door. 'No problem.'

Matt strode to her. He could feel Carl's eyes following him, and could almost hear the barrage of questions he'd be grilled with. He had a job to do, damn it. He'd made that clear at the start but still he was lumped with this sordid business.

He swallowed hard. He didn't want to do this, face her, confront what he'd done—no matter what the reason!

The set of her chin suggested a stubborn streak and the way she held her head high gave him the distinct impression she was going to meet him head-on.

This was not the deal. He fixed the woman with his business glare. Maybe he could just scare her away.

She didn't flinch.

Her green eyes were brilliantly intelligent, meeting his in blazing anger.

Cassie was furious. Furious with herself for getting into this mess and extra furious with this Matt guy for his part in it.

So Matt Keegan was handsome. The way he was looking at her right now wouldn't have induced her to have fallen into bed with him, much less anything else. His eyes were dark and his mouth pulled thin.

'Look, miss, I'm a busy man,' he said in his smooth, deep voice.

She bristled. 'Not busy enough, the way I see it. You have a responsibility.'

'Really?' He stood still, his back rigid, folding his arms across his wide chest, the rich outlines of his shoulders straining against the fabric of his shirt.

'Yes.' She stood taller and fixed him with what she hoped was an icy glare.

'To do what?'

'To tell me where the hell I am, for one.' Cassie took a quick look, left and right, very aware of the scene she was causing. But heck. To hell with it. He deserved every gram of embarrassment she could dish out.

'On the bridge of a ship.'

'I gathered that. Thank you very much.' It had taken her ages to find the foyer and ages more to convince someone to take her to Keegan, once she'd worked out there was no way she'd find him wandering around the ship. 'Going where?'

'Heading for New Zealand on the maiden voyage of *The Pacific Princess*.'

'New Zealand!' Her wedding was five days away! If she missed her own wedding…she'd kill him. 'How long will that take?'

'The cruise is for fourteen nights and fifteen days, but feel free to throw in a couple of hours for good measure. I'd hate to be blamed for misinforming you.'

She took a deep calming breath. If that was all she would blame him for he'd be lucky, and delusional. A lot more blame was heading his way, whether he wanted to recognise it, or not. 'How long until we get to land again?' She crossed her fingers.

'Not until Thursday. Dunedin is the first port of call in New Zealand. The ship cruises right around the islands then heads back to Australia.'

He was matter-of-fact, almost indifferent. Had he no idea what the implication of last night's activities had for her?

Days were going to be wasted. But at least the cake was ordered, the invitations were sent and the church was booked. The reception rooms were secured and catered for, and her white wedding gown hung in her closet waiting. She hoped the bridesmaids had picked up their dresses. And she could catch a plane back to Australia as soon as they hit land.

She gnawed on her lip. At least everything would be fine for Saturday. This didn't have to be a disaster. She still had her friends helping co-ordinate her wedding, fine-tuning it, watching out for those little things that could go wrong.

Eva had surprised her the most. Cassie had never been that close to her, but she'd apparently taken charge and organised the entire hen-night for her. Even the male stripper. She bit her lip, trying to recall the details through her foggy brain. She couldn't recall meeting any other men at all. 'You're the stripper!'

Matt looked around him. 'I beg your pardon?'

A murmur of voices around them gave Cassie the distinct impression that Matt Keegan would have to do a lot of explaining. She couldn't help but smile.

'Well, he was the only guy at the party last night.' She sobered. 'How else did I meet you?'

He met her eyes. 'Look…what's your name?'

'Cassie Win—' She swallowed the rest. He didn't need to know her entire name. It was probably wise to keep it from everybody. That way, nothing could get out about this whole debacle.

'Look, Cass, I'm in the middle of something here.' He waved a uniform over. 'Can you take Miss Win to her cabin?'

The young man offered a small smile. 'Sure. Your number?'

'I don't have a number.' She turned and glared at Matt. How dared he shorten her name ad lib? And how dared he forget her lack of travel arrangements? 'I woke up in *your* bed, remember?'

Matt pulled at the collar of his shirt. 'Find Miss Win a cabin and put her there, will you?'

'I'm sorry, sir. The ship is all booked. If she doesn't have a cabin, then technically she's a stowaway.'

'Really.' Matt rubbed his chin. 'What do you do with stowaways? Make them walk the plank, do dishes…or just throw them overboard?' His cool eyes caught and held hers.

Tension rippled through her.

The officer darted glances between them. 'Unless she's your guest?' he suggested, a tinge of hope evident in his tone.

Cassie fixed Matt with stormy eyes, waiting for his response. He was conspicuously silent. She bit her lip and counted to ten, giving him the benefit of the doubt. After all, she'd chosen *him*—even in her drunken state—to spend the night with. He couldn't be *that* bad.

The seconds passed. He couldn't possibly be so heartless and cold as to not feel any obligation, concern or anything else in between for her. She'd woken up in his bed! But there was no way she was going to tell the world about it. She'd rather forget it herself. No matter what the consequences.

She took a deep breath. 'Thank you, Mr Keegan, for your support,' she bit out sarcastically, 'but I'm sure I'll manage fine on my own.' She'd be damned if she'd beg for anything!

Cassie threw her chin high. 'Come on.' She yanked the young officer's arm. 'I need to make a call.'

Matt stepped in front of her. 'To whom?'

She shot him a withering glare. 'My fiancé, Sebastian, though it's really none of your business at all. You've made it abundantly clear where *you* stand. He'll get a chopper or something to get me off this bucket of bolts. No offence,' she tossed at the officer beside her.

'Fine.' Matt moved closer, reducing the distance between them and looking down at her. 'You go tell him what's happened—suits me fine. Goodbye.'

Cassie faltered, squashing the onslaught of nerves in her belly. What *would* she tell Sebastian? That she'd got blind drunk and fallen into another man's arms? How had she drunk that much anyway? She'd only had a couple of drinks and that cocktail Eva had got her to try. She chewed on her fingernail. Should she tell Sebastian at all?

There was always one talkback show or another discussing the subject—to tell or not to tell, that was the question. If you blurted out the whole story there was a chance he'd accept it, but he could bring it up at every argument, use it as an excuse for his behaviour, or it could fester just below the surface for years. But then he could just straight out dump you. Dump *her*.

She shook her head, trying to clear the residual thrumming of her headache. She couldn't ignore that she needed help. She glanced up, saw Matt's smug look and swung on her heel. She'd be damned if she'd give him any satisfaction, the dirty, rotten charmer. She strode down the hallway. *He* wasn't going to be of any help.

Her family would be of no help either. She ran through their itinerary in her mind. Her mother wasn't flying in from Europe until Friday night, her father from New Guinea Saturday morning, her younger brother was still in England on business and her other brother, Gary, was in America. There were a couple of friends she could call on, but she'd hate to burden them with a situation that they weren't able to help with. They just weren't equipped with the connections or the money to help her out of this one. She sighed deeply. She was on her own.

She matched the strides of the uniform beside her and she fisted her hands. Matt Keegan was acting as if he hardly knew her. How had she ended up with him? Cripes. There was absolutely nothing going for him. His generous build was forgettable. *And* his dark eyes. *And* that sexy, smart mouth of his. Nope. Nothing at all worth remembering. And she didn't.

'Here are the phones, miss.' The officer gestured to the bank of telephones and settled in at a discreet distance from her, but he was obviously keeping an eye on her.

Cassie's belly knotted at the idea she was akin to some criminal. As far as she was concerned it was she who was the victim, of sorts. It should be Keegan under watch, not her! She sighed. The world was definitely off kilter today.

She stared at the phone. She knew who she had to call and she wasn't comfortable with the idea, but she had very few choices left available to her.

She hesitated, gripping the receiver tightly. Her finger stiffly dialled enquiries and got connected. She didn't know if it was the right thing to do, but she couldn't think of anyone else.

One ring…two…three. 'Yes.' Eva was breathless.

'It's Cassandra Winters. I was wondering if you could do me a favour. I sort of fell asleep on that liner last night and now I'm at sea.'

'You are? My God. How did you sleep through it setting sail?' She paused a minute. 'You want me to tell Sebastian?'

'No. No. I figure I could do with a break for a couple of days and sort some things out. Just let him know I'm fine. I'll talk to him when I get back.' She'd have plenty of time to work out what she was going to say to him…it totally eluded her now. 'Could you feed my cat? You still have my spare key?'

'Sure. Anything wrong?' Eva's voice regained its usual silkiness. 'Do you want to talk about it?'

'Probably nothing more than wedding jitters…'

'O-kay. Are you sure? If there's anything else at all, any time, you can tell me.'

'Actually, I need you to send my passport and credit card to the Dunedin port so I can get off the ship. They're in the top left drawer of the bedroom dresser.' It was the best place to hide her plastic. There was no chance she'd hit the limit because she carefully considered every credit purchase. There were no temptations at passing sales—no card, no problem. And the card was there if she happened to get plastered, lose her purse and wake up in some strange bed.

Cassie crossed her fingers. 'I know it's a lot to ask but if you could, I'd be so grateful.' She was sure it would cost her when she got back. For all of Eva's kindness, she always had the feeling that there was a catch involved.

'Sure, I can do that. Keep in touch.' Eva hung up.

Cassie turned and faced the waiting sailor. She wasn't going to pussyfoot around the issue. The facts were the facts. She had no ticket, no cabin and no knight in shining armour. 'Where are those dishes?'

The uniform tapped his ear where a small cord ran into it. 'Mr Keegan says if you would have lunch with him at one-thirty in the Royale restaurant, he'll discuss the situation with you.'

A glow of satisfaction warmed her. So he'd come round… About time! Someone should give him a lesson or ten in manners and responsibility.

'Good.' Cassie couldn't help but smile. 'I have a good many things to say to him, too.' And none of them were suitable for sensitive ears.

CHAPTER FOUR

THE dining room was grand. Cassie held her hands tightly in front of her as she stared through the glass doors. She couldn't shake the unfamiliarity of the whole set-up or the fact the ship had several restaurants, and she could be making yet another mistake even meeting with the guy.

The ship had nine decks and it had taken her some time to find the Royale. Although she knew this restaurant was the one, it didn't help her confidence any. She dragged in a long, slow breath. And it had nothing to do with seeing *that* man again.

She cast a glance at her watch; one twenty-nine p.m.—right on time.

The timber floor in the Royale restaurant was polished within an inch of its life. The lighting was soft and the background music was gentle, yet lively, complementing the spirit of relaxation and fun that seemed to pervade on the ship.

It would have been nice to soak up some of the atmosphere, but there was no way. Not when she had the guilt of being some sort of freeloader hanging over her.

Cassie just wanted to hide, to crawl into a nice warm nook somewhere and forget everything. But there was no forgetting her wedding. She'd been waiting all her life for her perfect day. Had it all planned since she was fourteen. Adding details and fine-tuning designs, stationery, and dresses as the years had passed. It had been the one thing that she'd been able to hang onto. That one day, she was going to get married and her life would be perfect.

Everything was going to be as she'd always dreamed, except for the extra one hundred guests of Sebastian's, and the press, and the fact she'd slept with someone else five days before the wedding.

Cassie hesitated at the entrance to the busy venue. The place was packed with people. She couldn't help but smile at how the Hawaiian-shirt look had become an institution on cruises. There were so many happy faces, so much laughter and so many bright clothes.

She couldn't imagine her and Sebastian's honeymoon being so relaxed. Sebastian had organised a two-week tour of Europe. She figured they'd spend more time seeing, bussing and rushing than relaxing and enjoying each others company.

She combed her hair with her fingers, uncomfortably aware that she was wearing last night's clothes that had spent the night on the floor. She must look a fright. No make-up, no hairbrush, nothing but a watch, that said she was now twenty-five seconds late!

Cassie gave Matt's name to the attendant and was instantly whisked past the waiting guests to a table for two in the corner.

She sat down and reached for her napkin, her eyes

glued to the entrance so she wouldn't be caught off guard by Matt again. Her hand froze.

Matt Keegan strode in with all the force of a bull in a bad mood. His brows were drawn tightly together, his mouth pulled thin, his eyes stony. He yanked the chair out opposite her and sat down, waving the waiter over with a sharp flick of his hand.

'Well. Hello to you, too.' She leant on the table and tried to catch his attention. 'You're not a day person, are you?'

'You have no idea.'

'Enlighten me.' She tried to catch his eye, communicate with him on a deeper level. She needed to. To understand how on earth last night could have happened when her life had been so perfectly on course.

Matt's eyes were hooded. 'I'd rather we kept our relationship a formal one.'

Cassie raised her eyebrows. He couldn't be serious? 'That's a laugh, after last night.'

His eyes flickered. 'Yes. Right.'

Cassie had the insane urge to push him to say what lay behind his eyes. She had no doubt it was deep and important, but the words clogged in her throat. What if she'd done something, something during the night with him, that was…that was going to embarrass the hell out of her?

The waiter arrived, handing them each a menu.

Matt returned his to the waiter without opening it. 'A bottle of Riesling,' Matt ordered casually. 'And I'm after a light soup, then a lobster and salad.'

The waiter scribbled on his pad. 'And the lady?'

Cassie pursed her lips. Her stomach groaned its interest at his choice but she was painfully aware of not only being luggageless and roomless, she was also purseless. 'I'm afraid the lady is at the mercy of the gentleman's kindness.'

'Oh?' Matt looked taken aback for a moment. 'Order whatever you want. It's the least I can do.'

She raised an eyebrow. 'Indeed.' The very least, in fact. If she had it her way he'd be begging forgiveness on his knees. With his wide eyes staring up at hers, his large hands clasped together and his deep voice begging her pardon for what he'd done. Her mind seized. What if it had been her who had pushed for the interlude last night? Her cheeks heated. She turned her attention to the waiter, hoping that Matt Keegan didn't notice. 'I'll have the same, please.'

The waiter left them in an uncomfortable silence. It was even more awkward than being with a complete stranger. They'd skipped that step of politeness and interest, of 'liking', and gone straight to bed. It seemed almost ridiculous now to feign the niceties.

Matt began to drum his fingers against the table.

'So how do you suppose I not only came to be in your bed this morning—?'

His fingers froze. He lifted his head, his eyes wary.

She had his attention. 'But with nothing with me but the clothes on your floor, on my back, I mean…?' Her cheeks flooded with fire.

He put a hand up. 'Relax, please.' He snatched his napkin off the table and placed it across his lap, avoiding her eyes. 'There's no point going into the details. I'm afraid I don't have any answers.'

She darted a glance at him. She found *that* hard to believe, and way too convenient. 'You were drunk, too?'

Matt shrugged. 'I don't remember much at all.'

'But you said…?'

He sighed. His eyes roamed over her face, her eyes, her lips, down her long neck, and down.

Cassie's pulse skittered and she had the urge to hide the thrust of her breasts from his eyes. 'Okay. So you can remember some things,' she snapped. 'So typical of a man.'

He put up both hands in front of him, a devilish look in his eyes. 'I won't ask.'

The waiter returned with the wine. He bowed perfunctorily and displayed the label to Matt. Matt nodded and the man filled their glasses.

Cassie took a sip of the wine. 'At least I have good taste.'

'Pardon?' Matt put down his glass, his eyes widening.

'I picked a very important man, even if he is a jerk.'

Matt coughed. 'A jerk? Why exactly am I a jerk? For noticing a beautiful woman?'

'No, for walking out this morning like you did. For using your charms on me when I was obviously out of it.'

'Not a chance.' He shook his head.

'Then why can't I remember?'

He sat forward and looked at her intently. 'I have no idea. Have you got any medical conditions?'

'No.' Cassie glared at him, clenching her hands by her sides so she didn't do anything stupid. 'And what makes you such an important guy round here, anyway?' Everyone seemed to know his name, from the officers attending the foyer desk to the waiters in the restaurant.

'I have work on the ship. Let's leave it at that, shall we? No need to pry into each other's lives.'

'Yes, heaven forbid we get familiar.' Cassie's blood heated. 'You might actually have to consider feeling guilty over what you've done.'

He stiffened. 'It takes two to tango.'

She gulped some of the sweet white wine. 'And just how much tangoing did we do?' As soon as the words spilt out she wished she could snatch them back. She didn't want to know. Not really.

Thankfully, the waiter arrived. He placed a bowl of steaming hot soup in front of each of them.

Matt picked up his spoon and took a mouthful.

Cassie couldn't help watch his reaction. He hadn't even asked what soup they were serving. 'Well?'

'What?' Matt looked up innocently.

'What sort is it?' She hoped it was something he was violently allergic to and he'd bloat or go red or just break out itching.

He shrugged. 'No idea. It tastes good. Sort of creamy.'

Cassie looked to the waiter. 'It's cream of asparagus and cauliflower,' the man said with great pride.

Matt raised his eyebrows at her, and shrugged.

Honestly. Men. Didn't he care what flavour it was?

Didn't he care who she was and the implications of what he had done with her? She filled her mouth with the smooth soup in an effort to quench the uprise of disgust with Matt Keegan in her stomach. One spoonful after another, after another. She broke her bread and bit down hard, focussing on chewing and swallowing rather than the ache in the back of her throat.

'You haven't eaten in a while, I take it?'

She looked at him.

He was watching her, his spoon lying forgotten in his bowl, his eyes deep and dark and dangerous.

She stared into her soup. 'The only thing I've had this morning is a hell of a shock and a red rose. Neither was edible.'

Matt coughed deeply, and picked up his spoon again. He avoided her eyes and seemed intent on his bowl.

'Nice touch.' She looked up and stared at him. 'That rose. Really romantic.' Her throat threatened to close. 'I could almost think you have a heart.' She was fishing and she hated herself for it. It was just one night. It meant nothing, to her or to him.

The waiter arrived with the main dish, moving between them seemingly unaware of the friction. The scent of the hot lobster wafted upward, filling Cassie's senses. She'd only had it once before, with Sebastian. She stared at the colourful salad adorning the side contrasting with the shell. What would *he* think about her disappearing like this?

'Are you okay?' Matt's voice was warm and gentle.

She nodded and shook off the mood. 'So, what's the story?' She loaded her fork with salad, ignoring the tremor of uncertainty. 'Am I going to be spending the next three days in the kitchens and sleeping in some corner of some floor somewhere or are you going to find it in your heart to be a gentleman?'

'Well, when you put it that way... Okay, so you may believe I owe you something.'

She raised her eyebrows and bit down hard on some celery.

'All right. I'll see what I can arrange.'

'Thank you. Your mother would be pleased she raised you with some sort of conscience, however slow.'

'Kindly keep my mother out of it.'

She pursed her lips together. 'A little touchy on the family side, are we? Do you want to talk about it?' She paused. Watching Matt tackle his lobster. 'They got divorced, did they?'

'No. They did not,' Matt answered defensively. 'They've been happily married for forty years.'

Cassie's had *appeared* happily married until she'd turned eighteen when they'd been quickly and efficiently separated and divorced. 'Still happy?'

'Yes.' He placed his hands by his plate. 'Look, I told you, I'm not going to discuss my personal life with you.'

'Fine. Then I won't tell you about mine.' She took another load of salad. 'You're probably just insecure.'

'About what, I might ask?'

'About my family having much more successful careers, higher IQs and a far higher social position.' She lifted her chin. It was one thing she could say about her family. They were successful, but they were workaholic perfectionists and any time they spent together was scheduled, timed and maximised for efficiency.

Matt met her gaze. 'Personally, I don't find those elements defining. Are they happy?'

Cassie dropped her attention to her meal. She grabbed her glass and took a gulp of wine. No, they weren't happy. But who was? The occasional person in the street who was high on one substance or another. A mother with a new baby in her arms before reality set in. A person finding a new lease of life only to realise he brought himself with him.

She caught herself. That was her parents' talk. Not hers. Being brought up by a couple with doctorates in science and mathematics didn't give her any advantages, despite what her parents said. So they had money, they had position and brains—there was more to life. She was sure of it.

'Hit a sore point?'

'Not at all.' She managed a smile, shirking the familiar wave of insecurity.

They ate the rest of their meal in silence. It was a deepening one. One where the longer she remained silent the harder it became to break it. To find something to say. To connect again, even if it was just banal and meaningless.

Cassie laid her fork across the remnants on her plate and wiped her hands on the hot napkin the waiter had provided. She looked up. Matt was watching her again. She tossed the napkin on the table. 'So, I'll hear from you…some time soon about the room?'

'No.'

She darted a look at him. His warm dark eyes were

scrutinising her, the golden flecks in them looking brighter. 'But you said…?'

'You'll come with me to make the arrangements.' He rose in one fluid motion and straightened, smoothing out his black trousers. 'And you'll need some clothes.'

Cassie opened her mouth. No words came out.

'But don't think I'm getting a heart. I just don't want you coming and interrupting me again while I'm working.'

She stiffened. Typical. She stood abruptly, shooting her chair back into the wall behind her. 'Then why don't you go back to your precious work and forget all about me?'

He gestured for her to go first and followed her out of the restaurant. 'Because, as you pointed out before, my mother did raise me well and I'd rather know you have everything you need.'

There was no illusion he was doing it for *her*. 'So I don't pester you,' she stated, feeling his eyes on her.

'Exactly.'

Cassie bit the soft flesh on the inside of her mouth. She didn't want Matt Keegan's charity—she wanted far more. She wanted to see him apologise. She wanted to know he'd think twice before sweeping the next woman off her feet and into his bed. She wanted justice. Pure and simple.

CHAPTER FIVE

MATT KEEGAN leant back in one of the lounge chairs in the boutique. He couldn't say he'd ever had a more disagreeable woman in his midst. Or a more captivating one.

Cass was in a pair of designer jeans and an impossibly small white vest top. They hugged her curves to perfection and his body warmed as she walked toward him.

She threw out her arms. 'Like it? Good. I'll take it.' Her brilliant green eyes narrowed. 'This is on the strict arrangement I pay you back as soon as I get home.'

'Sure.' He let his eyes wander over her again. He'd always wondered what it would be like to play the benefactor to some damsel in distress. And it felt damn great, putting aside that he'd caused the distress in the first place. 'You'll need some formal wear for the evenings.' Matt found the idea of her parading gowns for him very appealing indeed. 'There's a dress code after six.'

'Great.' She tossed a look skyward. 'Just great.'

'I thought most women loved shopping?' Matt smiled. He couldn't imagine a woman that didn't. Probably because he hadn't yet met one, but as people said just because you haven't seen it yourself doesn't mean it doesn't exist.

'I do. With my own money,' she said, her voice strained. Cass ran a hand over some of the clothes racks, plucking out a couple of black dresses. She cast him a look of pain, then disappeared back into the changing rooms.

Matt clamped down on the surge of desire rushing through his veins. This woman was in love with someone else and was not available in any possible stretch of the imagination. She was off limits.

He'd met more women than he cared to admit. Gone out with half of them and hadn't found anyone that rang his bells, that set sirens going in his brain, that made the world move. Matt figured love was a figment of one too many poets' imaginations—and society had been sucked into the con of a lifetime. And Cass was just another woman, albeit an extremely interesting one.

Cass leant out around the corner, keeping her body shielded by the wall. 'Do I really have to show you?'

'If I'm paying…' He raised an eyebrow, hoping he was projecting a lazy interest rather than the thrum of anticipation that was making his head, and everywhere else, ache.

Cass stepped out.

Matt held his breath. Besides, there was no harm in looking at a pretty woman. And there was no doubt, Cassie Win was pretty.

The black backless gown she wore sent a sizzle of awareness pulsing through his veins, urging his body to needs, prompting him with mad images of taking her into his arms and crushing his mouth to hers. He shook his head and tried focussing on something else, somewhere else but his eyes wouldn't stay away— they kept coming back to Cass.

She ran a hand down her rounded hip, tilting her head to one side, revealing the creamy expanse of her neck as she perused her image in the full-length mirror along the far wall. The laugh she shot at her reflection struck him right in the chest.

Cass froze. She turned to him slowly, her eyes burning with reproach. 'These clothes are not some pay-off for services rendered,' she bit out.

Matt put up a hand, warding off her anger. He didn't like the way she could read him so easily. Was his attraction to her that transparent? 'Never occurred to me.'

'Good.' She gave him a hard second look, then relaxed. The gown clung faithfully to her every curve, from her calves to her voluptuous breasts. 'What do you think? Too much?'

Matt swallowed hard and spun his finger in a circle, indicating she turn for him. Damn, he was into torture. And such sweet, creamy torture she was.

His eyes feasted on the expanse of naked flesh she was showing as she gave him a perfunctory twirl. Her shoulder blades, the curve of her spine, the soft skin that beckoned for his touch, his lips…

Matt caught himself. He'd seen more of her in the cabin this morning and he'd walked away then. No need to get worked up now. She was just another woman. 'Looks good,' he said as calmly as he could manage.

Cassie turned to the shop assistant, trying to shirk the shivery feeling deep in her belly. 'I'll take this one, too.' She didn't want to know the price. She'd probably die. But she'd rather get a loan and pay it off over the next five years than admit any weakness in front of Matt Keegan.

'There you are.' A woman's voice jarred her out of her reverie. Cassie turned.

She was beautiful. Her eyes were midnight black, like her long hair, her skin sported a tan that Cassie and every other pale-fleshed woman on the planet would die for. She wore a smart trouser suit and a not-too-impressed look on her face.

Matt turned, recognition plainly on his face. 'What are you doing here?'

'I could ask the same of you. You should be working. Not chatting up the guests.' She had a silky voice and used her body as she walked closer to Matt—you couldn't ignore her.

'I had a little business on the side.' Matt stood up and straightened his shirt.

'And I can see exactly which side that would be.' She cast a dubious look at Cassie. 'And clocking up your credit card for you too, how lovely. I expected a bit more intelligence from you, Matt, of all people.'

Cassie couldn't move. She could hardly breathe. She struggled to find the significance of this woman and her words over the rush of blood to her face, pounding through her ears. Who was she?

'Thanks for your concern.' Matt leant over and kissed the woman on her cheek. 'But I've got this all under control.'

Cassie held her breath. Under control. *She* was under control? She dug her nails into her palms. Quite the contrary. She was way out of control and it wouldn't be long before she showed Matt Keegan just how far a compromised, trapped woman would go.

The woman raised her eyebrows. 'I'll talk to you later, then.' She turned and sauntered from the room, not even giving Cassie a second look.

'I'll see you at dinner,' Matt called after her, watching her stylish roll of her hips.

The black beauty lifted her hand, every fingernail finely manicured and painted a rich red, and continued on her way.

Matt turned. He almost looked disappointed that she'd left so quickly. Cassie's stomach clenched tight. 'Who was she?' The words tumbled from her mouth.

He shook his head. He ignored Cassie and looked to the assistant. 'I'll have to leave you ladies to take care of the rest. Unfortunately, I'd better go and get some work done.'

'Fine.' Cassie turned away, biting down on the barrage of retorts fighting for release. She didn't care who that fine-looking beauty was. She didn't care that Matt didn't want to tell her. She didn't care about anything except getting off this ship and getting back to Australia to get married. She glanced behind her.

Matt signed a slip at the counter, turned and strode out of the shop with such force and purpose—without even giving her a glance, or a goodbye—that she knew exactly what motivated him. Catching up with that woman. Cass should buy out the shop to spite him!

She pushed open the changing room door and shirked off the dress. She kicked it into the corner of the stall. So what if he had women falling all over him? He was nothing to her. Nothing but a bad memory she didn't even have.

Cassie sat in the library, staring at the pages of a book. Her new clothes were bundled up in carrier bags on the chair on her left but they were no comfort. She couldn't even bring herself to go crazy on Matt's credit card, knowing there was no way in the world she could live with herself if she didn't pay him back. And there was no way she could afford to pay off a vengeful shop.

The minute digit on her watch flicked over. It was five-o-five p.m. She was so alone. Cassie cast a long look around the couples nestled in the plush seats, whispering over their books. Happy faces. Sharing. Caring. She shifted her position in the chair. The only person she knew on the whole damned ship was a womanising jerk.

She swallowed a lump of self-pity and turned another page. She stared at her empty ring finger. She didn't even have her engagement ring to remind her of Sebastian. He insisted it stay in the safe except for special occasions, like for his press interviews.

Sebastian felt a million miles away. She'd be happy

to have just one of his campaign flyers to remind herself what a wonderful match they made together.

Cassie couldn't imagine exactly what life would be like as a politician's wife, in the public eye. But she was sure she'd adapt, with some time and organisation.

She rubbed her cheek with her hand, closing her eyes. She wanted to lie down somewhere and sleep, sleep away this whole darn mess and pray that when she woke up it'd all be only a dream that had never really happened.

If Matt hadn't been in such a rush to get away from her and catch that beauty, she would've had her room by now. She could have done with holing up in a darkened room for the next three days. Stuff the atmosphere, the opportunity to live it up on the luxury liner, the way she felt she wouldn't come out until they hit land.

She felt like throwing something.

Men were pigs. They really were. Since she'd met Tom in her final year of high school, men had gone out of their way to drive the fact home. She hadn't had a good run with men until she'd met Sebastian. She thanked the heavens she'd run into Sebastian in the car park, literally. Having to swap insurance details for the damage done to his Saab would never have occurred to her as the ideal way to meet a guy. But…they were so well suited to each other. It was fate. As Sebastian often said to her, they looked the perfect couple.

Five forty-five p.m. The minutes crept by slowly.

If only she'd worked out how long a minute was before, she could have fitted so much more into her schedules, and those of her clients.

How her staff were handling this turn of events, she didn't know. She'd rung earlier, informing her secretary of her situation, and she'd sounded quite confident with relaying the message and coping. She took a deep breath. They had to take on more responsibility some time. Although later would have been far more preferable than sooner, as far as Cassie was concerned.

She'd worked so hard on getting her time-management consultancy up and running it was a surprise to everyone, and her, that she'd had time for romance at all. She was lucky Sebastian was so... understanding.

She'd never forget his proposal. It was as if he'd been reading her work-notes. It had appealed to her. It had been at a lovely restaurant, with a bunch of red roses and a violinist in the background. It had been efficient. Short and sweet and to the point, without all that 'flowery nonsense'—as Sebastian called it. He'd given her all the reasons why she was perfect for him and vice versa. How could she have said no?

'Hi.'

Her heart jolted at Matt's voice, already annoyingly familiar to her. She opened her eyes slowly, gritting her teeth against the urge to sit bolt upright and scream. If he was going to ignore *her* and dump her, she'd damn well show him she didn't care.

He was crouched in front of her. His rusty brown

hair was unruly, as though he'd spent the last couple
of hours running his hands through it, or someone else
had. Her stomach tightened.

She couldn't miss that his jaw sported the slightest
shadow now and she had the insane urge to run a
hand along the bristles. Or slap them.

'You okay?' His voice was deep, smooth and
edged with concern.

She straightened. Her mind clearing. 'Yes. Of
course. I'm fine. Still feeling the effects of last night,
I guess.' Yes. That was it. That explained this almost
surreal feeling about her experiences today and why
her mind was flying off on disturbing tangents about
Matt Keegan.

'How's the book?'

'Book?' She looked down at the open text on her
lap. 'Great.' She hoped he didn't take it and ask her
what it was about. She had no idea. 'You've been
busy?'

'A good man is always busy.' Matt stood up and
shoved his hands into his pockets. 'I wondered, if
you're not doing anything for dinner you might like
to join me?'

Her mind warred with the idea. He was meant to
have dinner with that black-haired beauty. He'd even
chased after the woman. Had he shafted her? Or had
she refused him? Was Cassie a second choice? It
didn't matter. She couldn't show him how much of a
jerk he was long distance.

Cassie flicked through an imaginary planner. 'Yes.
I could squeeze you in. Right between sitting and

reading a dull book for the last two hours and jumping off the boat to swim back to Australia.'

He rewarded her with a smile.

It sent tingles of pleasure racing along her spine. 'And I'll need the energy,' she added as her stomach growled in agreement.

'Though you'll have to wait a couple of hours after you eat. Before you swim. Unless you plan on drowning.'

His eyes smiled at her and it was as much as she could manage to keep her mind on her goal and not on how nice it would be to remember exactly, in every glorious detail, what she'd done with him.

Cassie looked at her empty palm. 'No. Drowning isn't listed here. Looks like you're stuck with me for a few more hours yet.'

He held out his hand for her. 'I think I can manage.'

Cassie looked at his large, square hand. The long fingers, the strength inherent in them, the delights they would have shown her body last night. She snatched up her shopping and dumped a parcel in his offered hand.

'I need to change somewhere.' Cassie stood up. She was already painfully aware of the time but she glanced up at the clock on the wall to drive home the fact to Matt—six-twelve p.m. 'In your rush back to work this afternoon you forgot about the room.'

'The room…yes.' Matt plunged his hands into his pockets and looked around as though he was looking for a distraction. 'Come back to my cabin. You can change there.'

She shook her head, looking up into his face. 'Thanks, but I'd prefer my own.' There was no way on the planet that she'd set foot back in *that* room.

'I can understand that.' He turned and set off at a stride.

Cassie stood a moment, clutching her other bags in her arms, resisting the urge to follow the guy. She hadn't exactly come off very well in any of her interactions with Matt Keegan... But he owed her. She urged her feet to follow. 'I want to go to *my* room.'

'But my room is close and we're running late already for dinner...I promise to be a complete gentleman.'

'Rather than the man you were last night.' She bit her lip. He hadn't missed the meaning behind her hesitation. Damn. She didn't want him to think she was scared of him.

Matt faltered, casting her an open, honest look. 'I promise. I'll keep my hands to myself.'

Cassie followed him. Half of her wanted to run the other way as fast as she could, the other was drawn to complete what she'd started, on her terms. And that meant answers. 'You didn't say who that woman was earlier?'

'Didn't I?' Matt didn't slow down.

'No.' Was revealing who that beauty was so distasteful to him? Surely, he'd have no hesitation warding her off if she was going to step on his romantic interests and mess them up for him. Hmm. It didn't sound like a bad idea. She wondered if the beauty had any idea that Matt had been up to a lot more than shopping with her. 'Are you avoiding telling me?'

'Yes. It's none of your business.'

'Fine.' Cassie stuck her nose in the air and increased her pace. If he wasn't going to give her any rope to hang him with, she'd have to find her own.

Matt opened the door of his cabin.

Cassie hesitated. Who'd blame her? This guy had already turned her perfectly ordered life upside down and inside out. And this was the scene of the deed. She stepped in, willing her legs to co-operate.

She stared towards the bed. It had been made up, thankfully. Matt tossed her parcel onto it and went straight to the cupboard, appearing unperturbed by the close quarters and any memory of what they'd done.

Matt swung the cupboard doors open and took out a black dinner suit. He wasn't kidding. He meant *formal*—formal.

Visions of him dressed in that suit invaded her mind, taunting her with images of how well it would hug his body, how nicely it would enhance his dark eyes, how utterly engrossing it would be to peel it off him.

'Is there a problem?' Matt met her eyes.

She glanced at the carrier bags, her cheeks heating. 'No. Just wondering if I got the right dress.' Or made the right decision to accept his company instead of dirty dishes. Somehow, the dishes sounded a lot safer…

'Trust me. It's perfect.' He smiled and hung the

suit on a hook on the wall. 'You don't mind if I shower first, do you?'

'No, of course not.' She almost choked. 'It'll take me a few minutes to get my gear organised.' And there was no way she wanted to spread her underwear all over his bed with those dark eyes of his taunting her the whole time.

He strode into the bathroom and shut the door.

Cassie sagged against the wall. Cripes. What a situation to be in. She tipped the contents of her carrier bags out and arranged what she needed in a neat folded pile on the end of the bed. She gathered up the rest and shoved them back into the bags and stood with them staring at the cupboards. Call her a neat freak, but the idea of tucking them into a corner chafed on her—what was she going to do with them?

The sound of the shower filled her senses. He was standing there totally naked. Only metres away. One thin wall between them. Cassie swallowed. Engaged. She was engaged. And her fiancé's name was…

The door swung open.

Matt stood with a towel wrapped around his waist, steam curling around him. His bare torso was a testament to male perfection—all tanned muscle, with a light scatter of chest hair. Cripes, as beautifully muscled as any woman could possibly want. Cassie's mind filled with the idea of running her hands over him. Her pulse skipped.

Rivulets of water dripped from his hair, down his neck and chest, over a taut belly to where the towel covered his hips. His legs were long and tanned. His

feet large and bare. It was all Cassie could do to drag
air into her lungs.

'Your turn,' he said easily and strode to the dresser,
a toilet bag in hand.

Cassie closed her mouth and found her voice.
'Thanks.' Sebastian was not built anything like this
guy. She dropped her eyes to the bundle in her arms.
'Where can I put…?'

He walked towards her.

She held her breath.

Fantasies of what she must have already done with
his body invaded her mind. How could she not remember a body like that? Running her hands over
those hard muscles, kissing his hot flesh…

Matt reached behind her and opened a drawer. The
fresh scent of him—an enticing mix of soap and
maleness—invaded her senses. 'Plenty of room in this
one.'

She was careful not to make contact with his body
and dropped the bags in the drawer whole, tucking
them down so the drawer would close. She was very
aware that if she unpacked she'd be settling into his
cabin. Somewhere she was not going to stay a moment longer than necessary.

'This doesn't mean anything, you know. I just like
things neat.' She straightened and her eyes came level
with his soft, sensuous mouth. 'I'll just…get my
stuff…shower.'

'Sure.'

Cassie swivelled away from him. His damned annoying casual approach was getting under her skin,

chafing at her sense of self. Why wasn't he as affected as she was? Didn't he have any residual sense of lust for *her*? Was what she was going through normal?

Cassie closed the bathroom door and took several deep breaths. This was not a good idea. She was engaged. To be married. She shouldn't be having thoughts or anything else about this guy.

She stripped off her clothes in record time and stepped into the shower. The water was hot and refreshing and did wonders in washing her thoughts clean again. For a few minutes anyway.

Cassie dried and slipped on the black dress. The fabric was like satin, clinging to her skin, as soft and smooth as silk. She stared at herself in the mirror. No purse—no make-up, no lipstick, nothing—just pure, unimproved Cassandra.

And she didn't care. Well, she hadn't earlier when she'd bought the toothbrush and paste. She hadn't cared what she looked like and didn't want to care! Sebastian wasn't here. She knew no one, so what did it matter? And she certainly wasn't going to make any effort for Matt.

She tried combing her hair with her fingers. No luck. 'Have you got a comb I could borrow for a minute?' She bit her lip. She should have bought a brush. She would, tomorrow.

'Sure.' His voice was muffled.

A knock on the door announced that the respite was over. Cassie opened the door and took the comb, noticing Matt's eyes roving over her. He'd shaven, his jaw looking smooth and sensual.

'That was quick.' His mouth curved with amusement. 'I thought women took longer to get ready.'

'Only when they have make-up and hair to do,' she snapped. Matt's black dinner suit looked even better on him than she could have imagined. It was cut to hug his shape perfectly and the effect was absolutely devastating.

Cassie's heart hammered against her ribs. She swung back towards the mirror and combed her hair vigorously. She didn't want to dwell on his body for a moment longer than necessary. She styled her short hair, sweeping it to one side, then handed him back his comb. 'Thank you.'

She stared at the comb as the exchange took place. It suddenly felt too familiar, too intimate to have used it. Something from him, that he'd probably used minutes ago. She darted a glance to his neatly combed hair and her stomach curled.

'I like your hair like that.' He took the comb.

'I wasn't asking.' She shot him a look out of the corner of her eye as she swept past him and retrieved her shoes from next to the bed. He wasn't going to get anywhere with her, ever again.

Cassie slipped her feet into her black heels and thanked the powers that be that she had worn black last night. They matched this dress perfectly. Her mind darted back home to her cupboard, to her white heels, or the red ones she sometimes wore and breathed a sigh of relief she hadn't been wearing them last night. The sports shoes she'd bought earlier would *not* suit this dress! She stamped her foot. What was she doing thinking about fashion, for goodness' sake? Her whole future with Sebastian was on the line!

'Ready?'

She straightened the dress, a bit too aware of the plunging neckline. 'As I'll ever be.'

Matt tightened the knot on his tie, smoothing down the collar of his white shirt. 'Hungry?'

She eyed him carefully.

He looked at her, raising an eyebrow. 'Meant strictly literally, with no connotations.'

'In that case, yes.' She took a breath. She was becoming paranoid now. 'About a room of my own…?'

Matt moved to the door, grasping the handle. 'As the officer said earlier—they're booked out. Not a single room is available.'

A chill seeped into her pores. 'So what am I meant to do?'

'There's a sofa in the sitting room.' Matt cast a thumb in the direction of the sofa in question. 'Looks soft enough.'

She stared at him. 'Me… In *your* cabin?' She put her hands on her hips and pursed her lips. What did he think? That she'd been born last week? 'A bit convenient, isn't it?'

Matt put up both his hands, probably to ward off her accusation. 'A strictly platonic arrangement, I assure you.'

'Right.' She fiddled with the neckline on her dress, lowering her lashes to hide her confusion. The sofa was definitely a better option than washing dishes in the kitchens and being treated like some criminal, but only just. 'Well, I'm warning you…I'm engaged. I'm off limits and I'm not drinking!'

He opened the door to the cabin and waved her through, his eyes dark and unreadable. 'Fine by me.'

Cassie stalked past him. The urge to shove his casual indifference back in his face threatened to engulf her. It was nice to know he didn't care one way or the other, but damned irritating he could dismiss her summarily. Wasn't she a woman? Wasn't she desirable? Was using her once enough for this arrogant son of a jackal?

She clenched her fists by her sides as she matched his stride down the hallway. She had her work cut out for her to get him to see the injustice of his night of pleasure with her. But she was up for the challenge. No matter what he threw her way!

CHAPTER SIX

THE Royale Restaurant took on a totally new look at night. The tablecloths had been changed to a deep burgundy over white, the lighting even softer, and bunches of carnations adorned the centre of each table.

Cassie was adamant that she kept her distance from Matt. She was resolute to stay well away from any alcohol and not to lose herself in his charms again. She might be stuck here for the next three days but it didn't mean she had to like it.

They wove between the tables and stopped at one already occupied. Cassie stiffened. A woman sat next to two males. One a very burly, very blokey sort and the other a light-framed, lanky man with glasses that seemed to balance precariously from the end of his nose. And the woman…the woman was the dark beauty.

She clenched her hands by her sides. It wasn't a matter of Matt choosing her over the black beauty. He was going for both!

The woman looked up. 'There you are. Thought you got lost.' She winked to the men beside her. 'Or something.'

Cassie's cheeks heated at the woman's insinuation and she stepped a little further away from Matt. It might have been the case last night but today was a different matter altogether, and there was no way she wanted to wear that particular label.

Matt leant down and kissed the woman on the cheek with an intimacy that twisted in Cassie's chest. What sort of relationship did he have with this woman? The woman had been dead jealous this afternoon when she'd seen Cassie with Matt. Why the change?

He cleared his throat. 'I'd like you all to meet Cassie Win. This is Carl, Rob and Trent.'

All eyes rested on her. Never had she wanted to crawl into a hole more. The black beauty was wearing a stunning strapless red gown that made the most of her ample assets. And the fact didn't seem to escape any man's notice at the table. Cassie smiled anyway. 'Nice to meet you. Sorry to intrude.'

'Nonsense.' The woman gestured to the empty seats. 'Sit down and relax. We don't bite, though Matt here has probably told you otherwise.'

Cassie would have liked to blurt that Matt hadn't told her anything about anything, but figured it would be an admission of her total lack of importance. Which suited her, but not in front of Black Beauty. 'I'm sorry, I think I missed your name.'

'Rob.' She tossed her dark mane over her shoulder. 'Robyn, actually, but everyone's too lazy to bother with the rest and I don't care…'

Cassie managed a smile. Matt pulled out a seat for her and she eyed him carefully, looking for any hint at what was going on between him and Rob.

He smiled.

Cassie's pulse jumped to attention and she narrowed her eyes, scanning his charming face. Was he up to something?

She warily sat down, keeping her attention fixed on Matt. If he was trying to convince her that he was in fact a gentleman he was doing a good imitation—his only failing the incident last night, and this morning's debacle.

The memory of last night had to come back to her eventually. Even trauma victims blocking out horrific experiences got flashes of what had occurred. And she expected that what she'd endured was far from horrific... Her cheeks heated, again.

Cassie lowered her gaze, concentrating on placing her napkin across her lap. She couldn't believe she was letting this get to her. She was twenty-four, for goodness' sake, way past teenage flushes and fits of embarrassment.

'Don't mind us. We're normal really.' Rob smiled at her, her eyes glinting, her voice all friendliness. 'Tell us all about yourself.'

Cassie stared into the woman's inquisitive face. Her fine features, her dark eyes with brilliant golden flecks and her manner gave no indication of duplicity. 'Not much to tell. I'm really boring.' She shrugged. 'What about you guys? What are you all here for?'

Matt poured Cassie a glass of cola from the jug on the table and topped up the rest of the glasses from the bottle of Merlot. It was disconcerting the way he kept glancing at her, how her eyes locked with his, repeatedly. *What was his problem?*

'We're here for work.' Rob took a sip of the red.

Cassie glanced at Matt. Judging by his appearance, his bearing, his sharp assessing stares, it had to be some white-collar work, behind some desk somewhere...

'But that's really dull. I just want to know where Matt managed to meet you. Did you know about the cruise and wangled a ticket to be near lover-boy here or—?'

'I think we'll stop prying.' Matt's tone was even, yet edged with steel.

'Come on,' Rob appealed to Matt. 'Throw me a titbit. I want to know who this *other* woman is.'

Cassie was right. Rob and Matt did have a relationship! She met Matt's hooded eyes and his cool warning look punched her directly in the chest. She wished she knew what was going on in his mind. And some idea of what was going on between her and him, and him and Rob, would have made life easier. But his warning was clear—don't tell.

Matt didn't want her to say anything? Well, tough! She wasn't about to let him control her! If she wanted to answer then she'd damned well answer and to hell with him. 'No, I wasn't expecting a cruise.'

'You surprised her? How romantic. Isn't that so romantic of him?' Rob glanced at the two men beside her who looked quite lost in the wake of her enthusiasm.

He'd surprised her, all right. But not in the way

anyone at the table could have imagined. Cassie cast him a piercing glare. God, she wished she knew exactly what had gone on that first night between them.

Matt averted his eyes. 'Have we ordered?'

The men beside Rob shook their heads, while Rob ignored the question and stared directly at Cassie.

Cassie shifted in her seat. It was as though Rob was trying to read her mind, to work her out—either way, there was no escaping the fact that this woman had a vested interest in Matt.

Matt raised his hand and signalled the waiter.

Cassie stared at the menu, her mind more interested on what could be going on between Matt and the beauty than food. Why in heaven would he risk a fling with her when he could have Rob any time he liked?

She ordered a starter of potato skins with sour cream, and grilled whiting with vegetables for mains, proud that her words came out cool, calm and sensible—everything she wasn't feeling right now.

Rob handed the menu back to the waiter. 'So, what do you do?' She propped her elbow on the table and cupped a hand under her chin, shooting Cassie an inquisitive stare.

'I'm a time-management consultant.' Cassie gripped her watch. She'd never gone so long without her planner. She stared across the room. She needed to get a pen and paper, to get some schedule in order. That would make her feel better. Safer.

Carl picked up his wine, brandishing his snake tattoo as he raised the glass to his lips. His short-sleeved shirt did little to interrupt the elaborate artwork climbing his limb. 'We could do with your services, couldn't we, Matt?'

Matt stroked the stem of his glass, not taking his eyes off Cassie. 'At times.'

Cassie looked away. She'd rather not watch him watch her. It was disconcerting. Disturbing. And detrimental to her concentration.

'Do you have family?' Rob gave an encouraging smile.

Cassie darted a look at Matt. It definitely annoyed him that she was getting friendly with his co-workers. 'Yes. I'm the youngest of three, the only girl. And you?'

Rob smiled and glanced at Matt. 'I'm the only girl, too. We were three once. But one of my brothers died.'

'I'm sorry.' Cassie took a breath and tried to centre herself. She glanced at Matt and he looked away, but the raw hurt that glittered in his eyes was unmistakable. She stared at her glass. For some crazy reason, talking to his friends didn't seem that important now, not if it hurt him like that.

'It was a while ago now. My brother took it the hardest. They were very close.'

'I can understand that.' Cassie couldn't miss the look cast between Rob and Matt. She wished she could read minds. She wanted to know more about these two. Lots more. They seemed to have a bond beyond words or looks. Cassie's throat constricted and she looked away. She clenched her hands tightly on her lap. She'd changed her mind. She didn't want to know!

Matt shifted awkwardly. 'So how did the job go today?'

Rob glared at Matt. 'You know all about work and you made us promise not to talk about it, so we're not.'

'Any pets?' Trent asked, his voice cracking and his ears turning a deep beet-red.

Cassie couldn't deny the man's effort to join in. 'I have a cat, Frizzle. She's a bit of everything but mostly a fluff ball.'

Matt scraped his chair backwards and stood abruptly. 'I could do with a bit of fresh air before I eat. I'll be back shortly.' He moved quickly, as though they were contagious.

Rob raised her eyebrows. 'What did I say?'

'I think it was me.' Cassie gripped the stem of her glass tightly. She couldn't help feeling responsible. If she hadn't got drunk…

He had to loathe being lumped with her, intruding on his life, on his time with his friends and cramping his style with this *femme fatale*.

She caught herself. What was she thinking? He was the A-grade jerk here. So what if she cramped his style. The more cramping the better!

Carl stood up, coughing deeply. 'Come on, Trent. Let's check out the action at the bar.' The men rose and headed to the bar, without looking back.

'We managed to scare them off.' Rob laughed and

leaned onto the table watching the guys as they wove between the tables. 'Lovers' tiff, hey?'

'No,' she blurted. 'It's not like that.' Cassie's heart pounded in her chest. 'Look, I'm not here to stand on anyone's toes. Matt and I aren't involved, you know.'

'Yeah, right.' Rob smiled.

'No, truly. I have no intentions at all in his direction. You have nothing to worry about.' Except maybe that her boyfriend was a number one jerk who played around behind her back, but she wasn't going to break it to her.

Rob laughed, then sobered. 'But…you do know…I'm his sister.'

'Sister?' The word stuck in her throat. It was obvious now. Rob's eyes were the same as Matt's, the skin the same rich tan… How could she have been so blind? 'No?'

'Hell, yes. What was he doing not telling you? Gosh, no wonder you've been put out. You've been jealous.'

'Me? Jealous? No.' Cassie shook her head. Not a chance. Why should she care who Matt was with or wasn't. Rob was just reading more into things because she knew Matt and his womanising ways.

Rob stood up. She grabbed Cassie's arm and pulled her out of her seat. 'Come with me.'

'Where?' She didn't want to go anywhere. The table was safe. Almost empty. And Rob wasn't Matt's lover. Why would she want to go looking for trouble?

She steered her out onto the deck outside. Cassie's eyes focussed on Matt leaning heavily on the rail.

'Oh, no. No,' she whispered harshly, backing away. 'I've nothing to say to him.'

'You know what they say. Don't let the sun set on a disagreement—well, it sounds like you two need to talk about it to me.'

Rob shoved her extra hard towards Matt and Cassie staggered to regain her balance and some composure. Great, just great! What in blazes was she going to say to him? She held her hands still in front of her. 'Thinking of jumping?'

'No.' He didn't turn. 'I was thinking of you.'

'Oh.' She moved to the rail, gripping the cold metal tightly and staring down at the water below. 'Of me jumping off? I guess it would be a lot easier if I just disappeared…'

He shot her a pained look. 'No. I was thinking of how hard I've been on you. And I want to apologise. I can't explain but I want you to know that I would never deliberately have set out to hurt you…'

Cassie stifled the swell of excitement in her belly. 'Look, don't start getting mushy on me now. You'll wreck this terrible opinion I have of you.' And Cassie desperately needed to believe he was the number one jerk to keep herself from falling off the path she'd set for herself. She had her future all mapped out. Sebastian and she were going to be married, have two children, settle down in Sydney's prestigious suburb of Double Bay and live happily ever after.

She stared at his hand on the rail, so close to hers yet so far. It wasn't meant to be. There was no room in Cassie's plan for a man like Matt Keegan.

Matt felt her close beside him, could almost feel her body heat. It was all he could do to continue to look casually out over the flat expanse of water, watching the night sky and the thousands of stars in the heavens. The moon's brilliance shone onto the water, adding to the effect, but all he wanted to do was confess.

Damn Rob couldn't keep her mouth shut. It had been much easier to ignore the implications of what he'd done when he hadn't known anything about her. Now, he was hopelessly aware that she was a lovely human being who didn't deserve it. All those stories he'd been fed about her weren't true. He ran a hand through his hair. Hell, he'd known it from the start, but anonymity had made it somehow easier. Now, he was sinking fast.

'You said you're engaged,' he said carefully.

'Yes. To a very nice man. Sebastian—'

'And you feel you're ready to make a lifelong commitment to this man?'

'You probably wouldn't understand,' she said haughtily. 'Being the way you are. Sebastian and I are perfect for each other.'

He ignored the personal jibe. How was he going to wake her up to reality? 'Are you sure?'

'Yes.'

Matt turned to her, and gazed into her face, watching the shadows of the clouds moving across the moon on her creamy white skin. 'Are you going to tell him what happened with us?'

She hesitated. 'Yes. I will. Because I know he loves me and he'll understand. It didn't mean anything.'

Matt clenched his jaw. Sebastian didn't deserve a woman like this. And she didn't deserve to be hurt and humiliated. If there was one thing he owed her, it was to show her what life really was like so she didn't go back to her fiancé, only to have her heart broken.

And somehow, he'd make Sebastian regret the day he'd blackmailed him into telling that nasty little lie to Cassie. And one way or another he'd make sure his plan failed.

CHAPTER SEVEN

'ROB is your sister,' Cassie said accusingly.

Matt turned to her, keeping his features impassive. 'Yes.' He shrugged and shoved his hands into his pockets, walking along beside her on the deck. He should have known two women together would break down the stranger barriers in lightning speed. Whatever else he did, he had to keep the two of them apart at all costs. It wouldn't do for Cass to find out exactly how they were connected to her fiancé.

'And you lost your brother,' she said softly.

Matt swallowed hard. It wasn't something he couldn't ever forget. 'Yes, my younger brother. It was a tragic accident.'

She laid a warm hand on his arm. 'How?'

'He drowned, okay?' Matt snapped, the words bursting from him, laced with the pain he carried.

Cass let her hand drop.

Matt faced her, sobering. 'I'm sorry. I didn't...' He dragged in a deep breath. 'Will you stop asking questions? I don't want you to know too much about me.'

'Why the heavens not?' Cass turned to him, her brilliant green eyes wide. 'We certainly got to know each other intimately last night. Why not fill in a few details for consciences' sake?'

'Because it was a mistake.' He ran a hand through

his hair and looked out to the starry sky, trying not to focus on her lovely face and the hurt behind her eyes. But he was drawn…

Her eyes dimmed, but she smiled. 'I agree. Biggest mistake I've ever made. One that I'm glad I can't remember.' She turned and kept walking.

They moved slowly up the deck in silence for a while, then Cass stopped, walked to the edge of the ship and gazed out over the water, leaning her elbows on the railing. 'Could you ask your sister if I could share her cabin with her?'

'Her cabin?' Matt looked at her. 'I could… But I don't know whether I want the two of you together talking about all sorts of things.' He knew he didn't.

She waved a hand dismissively. 'We already have.'

He swallowed a lump in his throat. How much could a couple of women talk about in ten minutes? He couldn't have been gone much longer than that. One thing for sure, she didn't know the truth. She wouldn't be standing next to him talking calmly if she did. 'I'll ask her, then.'

'Great.' She stared up at the stars.

Matt couldn't help but notice the way the light fell on her fine features, or the rose flush to her cheeks, the soft fullness of her lips, and the faraway look in her eyes…

Cass suddenly turned, catching him off guard.

'I meant *now*,' she said with a quiet, yet desperate, firmness.

He straightened. 'Yeah, sure. Okay.' He rubbed the unpleasant stiffness in his neck, hoping to hell she didn't read too much into him ogling her. She was a pretty woman. Nice to look at. That was all.

Cass raised a finely arched eyebrow at him, her eyes darkening.

Damn it. He hated people not having a good opinion of him. It chafed. It was against his nature to deliberately alienate someone. And boy, he'd done a good job with Cass.

Matt strode back down the deck and through the doorway. He scanned the restaurant. A waiter was placing steaming hot dishes onto their table. Rob, Carl and Trent were there. Rob noticed him first and waved him over.

He shot a look back at Cass walking slowly along the deck toward him. He had half a mind to leave her outside. Out of Rob's firing line and his personal space. He couldn't imagine what he'd been thinking inviting her to eat with his team. Probably that he'd get a respite from the guilt she evoked in him. Just his luck to have doubled the problem.

Matt exhaled sharply. She wouldn't be his problem much longer. Thank goodness. He'd grabbed an officer earlier and instructed him to arrange Cass a charter flight as soon as they hit Dunedin. Getting her to the nearest international airport and away from him as soon as possible was in his best interests, and Rob's, and, ultimately, Cass's too.

'Dinner has arrived,' Matt called back to her, then strode in alone. He'd told the man to secure her a plane ticket back to Australia as well. There was no way he was going to take any chances and get stuck with her for any longer than he had to.

He went straight to Rob's side and knelt down beside her, leaning close. 'Can you give the twenty questions a rest? Cass is pretty strung out.' He kept his face neutral. It was his best bet in getting the lie past his sister.

Rob patted his hand where it rested on the table. 'Sure. Not a problem. Things okay between you two now?'

'I'm working on it.' His sister might be very astute, but she was too concerned with matchmaking to bother reading him too closely. Thank goodness.

Cass entered the dining room. She wove between the tables with an easy grace, the black gown making her movements all the more sensual. He found himself extremely conscious of her appeal, of the glowing softness to her skin, and of how tight his trousers were.

It didn't escape his notice how many other men in the room noticed her, either. An ache deep in his gut caught him off guard.

Matt took a breath and leant closer to Rob. He had to concentrate on the job at hand. He racked his mind for the right question. He counted his pounding heartbeats until Cass had reached the table. 'Did you want to swap meals?' he whispered to his sister, knowing full well that the seafood platter she'd ordered was her favourite.

'No,' Rob said loudly. She flicked her napkin onto

her lap, tossing him a look of obvious dismissal. 'You're dreaming!'

Matt resisted the urge to smile. Just the answer he needed. There would be no way Cass would ask his sister now. Little chance she'd ask anyone else to share at all. He'd keep an eye on her now. And keep her safe.

Cassie pulled out her chair and sat down. Her eyes were on him, wide and concerned.

Matt stood and shrugged at her. She hadn't missed the performance. *I tried*, he mouthed wordlessly over his sister's head.

Cassie's hope dropped to the pit of her stomach. She concentrated on straightening her napkin on her lap and not on the deluge of doubt that threatened to swamp her. How was she going to survive in Matt's cabin?

It was obvious by her quick dismissal that Rob wasn't about to surrender her privacy to a complete stranger. Cassie didn't blame her. If *she* had a cabin of her own on this luxury liner she'd live it up too. She smoothed the creases out of the napkin, taking long deep breaths. She could imagine sharing with Cassie would cramp Rob's style.

She tried not to look at Matt again, but failed. She was so confused. She knew what had gone on between them last night, the evidence spoke for itself, so was she tempting fate by being anywhere near Matt? Would he try to weave his charms on her again? Her pulse raced at the mere thought of it. Did he *still* like her, or was she another slam-bam, thank-you-ma'am one-nighter for him that had just happened to stick around?

Cassie took a deep breath and a sip of her cola. She was a mature woman. Engaged. Controlled. Sober. She wouldn't have a problem in the world later with him alone in the cabin.

She gnawed on her lip and dragged her plate closer to her. The aromatic scent of the spicy potato skins tantalised her stomach. The ceramic dish with the starter sat upon a larger plate, adorned on the side with snow pea shoots and curls of carrots. A platter of assorted salads sat in the middle for the table to share. Cassie took a scoop of each.

Matt reached over, his cologne wafting to her. Cassie refused to meet his eyes; she didn't even deign him with a glance. There was nothing about him that could induce her to even like the man. The turmoil deep in her stomach was stress—that was all.

Cassie concentrated on the food. The tropical potato salad was a subtle combination of potatoes with banana, egg and finely chopped shallots in a creamy mayonnaise that caressed her taste buds. The kedgeree a light and refreshing mix of rice, onion, garlic, peppers and smoked salmon. And the rainbow coleslaw a colourful blend of cabbages with carrots, onions, apples and pine nuts.

Matt's presence by her side, almost touching her arm with his, dominated her senses. He was so close. Too close. His plate of oysters a vivid reminder of his total lack of consideration for her. What was he thinking eating something so blatantly aphrodisiac?

The table was conspicuously quiet. It suited Cassie not to talk, be asked questions or answer them—it was hard enough just to eat. The tension was probably going to give her a case of indigestion.

Her main dish was a mouth-watering piece of fish, topped with a chunky sauce of aubergines, peppers and onions, and garnished in parsley.

Cassie refused more cola. She didn't want to take any chances with any liquids—alcohol, caffeine or sugar. Matt looked so good in his dinner suit that she could almost imagine how she'd succumbed to his charms, in her drunken state.

Her eyes kept darting to the way his fingers, tapered and strong, caressed the stem of his wineglass and she couldn't help but wonder what they'd felt like, all over her body…

Cassie shifted in her seat. She couldn't stand much more of this tension. She darted a quick glance around the table while the waiters brought dessert. She wished someone would say something to relieve it.

She poked the crushed hazelnuts around the grated chocolate and cream on top of her rich, velvety mousse. The realisation that she couldn't fill the void inside her with food was sinking in. She took a heaped spoonful of the wickedly sweet dessert anyway. It melted in her mouth but did nothing to change anything other than her calorie count for the day.

Cassie ate slowly, watching Matt push the slivers of lime rind garnish to one side of the long stemmed goblet his dessert had come in. He sliced off a scoop of a mango and lime sorbet ball and took it to his mouth. She watched, mesmerised, as his mouth closed over the spoon. She raised her eyes to see if he liked it.

He was watching her.

Cassie swung away and watched two couples move onto the dance floor near the raised stage where the band played. She looked longingly at the way they wrapped themselves in each other's arms. She wanted that. She wanted comfort. She wanted someone's arms around her holding her close. She coughed away the dry ache in the back of her throat—Sebastian was over a thousand kilometres away.

She snapped her attention back to her dessert and scraped the dish clean with the edge of her spoon.

Rob leant forward. 'Do you—?'

'Dance,' Matt interrupted. He rose from his seat, tossing his napkin onto the table. 'Would you like to dance?' He held out a big, strong hand to her.

Cassie looked at it dubiously. She hadn't touched him since last night. Couldn't remember touching him at all. His hands were large and square, almost working-man hands but for the obvious flawlessness of them. She could imagine them being strong, smooth and sensual.

'Don't you dance?' he asked softly.

'Not well. I never learnt. It didn't seem important.' Her parents hadn't classed many things as important. Things that she'd had to improvise in since. Relationships. Sharing. Friends. More often than not they'd been tough things to learn later in life.

Her parents had been consumed with their own

busy careers, the only priority for their children had been their education. Extra lessons, tutors and study had been crammed into what time Cassie had left after school. Presents in her family had always been practical. Calculators, computers, reference books and science kits.

'Trust me.' Matt took her hand lightly in his.

Bolts of pure excitement raced up her arm and into her chest, sliding gently to her belly. His hands were as soft as they looked, strong yet gentle.

Cassie stood up. Her pulse skittered and her heart hammered in her ears. His heat scored into her flesh where his hand held hers, enclosed in his warmth, and it was all she could do to force her legs to hold.

Matt moved suddenly, turning and striding to the dance floor. Cassie had no idea if he felt the charge between them. It was probably just some remnant passion from last night's interlude.

Matt swung around, pulled her close to his warm, solid body and slid his other arm around her, resting his hot palm against the bare flesh of her back.

She willed herself to breathe. Her curves moulded to his contours, reminding her again of what they'd shared the night before. Her body must be remembering. Every inch of her was tuned to him and his sensual motion, to the touch where her skin met his, and to the rhythm of the music.

'Just move slowly, feel my legs and go with the flow,' Matt breathed into her ear, his voice deep and warm.

Cassie could feel his legs all right. His muscular

thighs were rubbing against hers in a way that reminded her again of what her body already knew they'd shared. *If only she could remember!* She could feel his every movement, felt his body under her hand, felt his pulse throbbing where their palms met. An annoying shiver coursed along her spine.

She moistened her lips. Was dancing always this close? Every time she'd been faced with dancing at a venue with Sebastian, he'd left her at the table, accepting of her ineptitude, choosing some lithe and graceful stranger instead.

The music was romantic, the melody slow, calling to Cassie's heart, taking her on a mental respite, where only her body and his were there.

The melody swelled and ebbed.

The spicy scent of his aftershave filled her senses, sending a giddy jolt of vitality snaking through her nerves. How was she expected to think clearly with him holding her so close, with his leg between hers, with his scent enticing her, with his warm breath on her cheek?

'Have you thought about your life? How you want it to be?' Matt's voice was warm, gentle.

'I stopped dreaming of knights in shining armour years ago, if that's what you mean. And castles in the air… No, I'll go for a condo on the beach.'

'You're motivated by money?' He sounded quite accepting, almost as though he'd anticipated her.

'No.' Cassie held her tongue in check. Gawd, she wanted him to choke on his prejudice! What did he think she was—a gold digger?

'You don't want to explain?'

'No.' She didn't even want to talk with him. How could he make her feel so much by just holding her? What the blazes had they done last night to warrant this wanton behaviour of her body?

She took a calming breath. Telling him more would further complicate things. After all, she'd never see him again after this nightmare of a cruise was over.

She sighed. 'I know that there's more to a marriage than financial security. Mutual interests, friends, goals all make Sebastian the perfect choice for me.'

'What about love?' His warm breath touched her face.

Cassie faltered, her foot coming down on his. 'Sorry.' She looked over his shoulder, her mind whirling over the connotations in his line of questioning. Did she want him that 'guilty' or did she want to keep her personal feelings just that—private and personal? 'Is that your sister over there? Wow, is she getting close or what?'

Matt jerked his head around. Rob was draped around a tall, dark and handsome Latin man, her body sliding against his in a very provocative dance.

'What the—?' Matt let her go abruptly.

There was no mistaking the look in his eyes. Attack. Cassie held onto his sleeve. 'She's a grown woman, you know.'

Matt hesitated. 'I'm not having her being used as someone's entertainment.'

'My, my, aren't we a giant hypocrite?' A swell of

indignation pulsed in her chest. If he'd acted even half the gentleman last night…

He folded his arms across his chest and glared at her, his eyes fierce. 'God, do you ever stop?'

Cassie moved closer to him, staring up into his dark eyes. 'No,' she said firmly. 'Just think of me as your conscience. A very determined one.'

'I noticed.' He started to turn again toward his sister.

Cassie grabbed his chin with her hand, holding it. 'You asked me about myself,' she blurted, trying to ignore the warm flesh beneath her fingers. 'You know I'm a time-management consultant, engaged to be married, and happy with the idea of financial security.'

Her body heated at the contact and the deep promise in Matt's eyes. She dropped her hand. 'So that's it. That's where I'm at, what I'm planning and where I'm heading.' And if he couldn't handle that then he could go to blazes.

Cassie tried not to look over his shoulder and bring attention to Rob again. She didn't want to be the cause of Matt racing over and crashing in on Rob's good fortune.

Matt grabbed her by the shoulders and pulled her closer to him. 'You can't do that.' His voice was edged with smoke, of a fire that smouldered in his eyes.

She found her voice. 'What?'

'Look at me like that, then not do anything, say anything to…'

'Tough.' She pulled out of his hold and looked over his shoulder again rather than in those dark eyes of his. The score changed and she offered him her hand, praying he'd accept it. She wanted to dance with him. Not get personal. Not get intimate.

'Life's tough,' he qualified, wrapping his hand around hers again, yanking her close and moving his body with the music.

'Don't I know it.' Heat radiated from him, sending frissons of electricity racing along her every nerve. Saving Rob's Latino love affair from doom was valiant, but not at any price. She edged away, creating a bit of distance between them.

'No. I mean it.' Matt relaxed his hold on her. 'People can be mean, selfish and cruel.'

'I forgive you…okay,' she blurted. The words were out before she could think and she instantly regretted them. She wasn't ready to forgive him for what he'd done.

'Me?' He pulled back and caught her eyes with his.

She licked her dry lips. How dared he be surprised? How could he act innocent and shocked? 'Yes. You were probably just taken by the moment and swept me off my drunken feet.'

He coughed. 'Yes, well.' He glanced at his watch. 'I think it's time for bed. I've got a long day tomorrow and some people have to work.'

She stiffened.

'Bed in a purely platonic way.' Matt guided them across the dance floor to the side in time with the melody.

'Fine. Of course.' She straightened tall and pushed down the unusual ache in the pit of her stomach. 'I can handle that. Can you?'

He moved his hand from the bare flesh of her back to her waist, before dropping his hand completely. 'Not a problem.'

Cassie glanced at him. That was it, then. As long as he wasn't lying.

CHAPTER EIGHT

CASSIE clenched her hands tightly in an effort to still the nervous energy in her body. She walked back to Matt's cabin with him, counting their steps with the pounding of her heart.

Matt hardly said two words and his inability to hold up any sort of conversation with her on the way didn't instil confidence in her about spending another night together. Apart. In the same room, but not the same bed.

Matt flicked the switch on the wall and strode into the suite without a hesitation. He strode through the sitting room and shirked his jacket off. He threw it on the bed, then started working his tie.

Cassie closed the door and flipped the catch. Habit. She stared at the lock and chewed her lip. She glanced at the way Matt filled the designer shirt, his muscles evident, his glorious body only a thin shirt away. She was used to locking out the bad guys. Tonight, she couldn't help but think she was locking herself in with one.

Somehow, she managed to face him.

Matt started unbuttoning his shirt. Cassie couldn't turn away. One button. Two. Three. Four. The shirt fell open revealing curls of hair on his tanned chest. He had to work out somewhere. There was no way the average suit could look that good stuck behind a desk all day. He had to go to some gym and work that body of his... She licked her dry lips.

Sebastian was a tennis man and there was no denying the fact that he didn't look anywhere near as good as Matt. They were a similar height, but that was where any likeness ended—Sebastian was thin, lanky and blond where Matt was...not worth her time thinking about.

Matt wouldn't be in any shortage of female company. His face was pleasant if not a little too handsome for her, and his body was okay, if you didn't mind all that tanned muscle.

Cassie kicked off her heels. She was hopelessly aware she still stood next to the door, her legs unwilling to take her into the room, closer to *him*.

She looked at the bed dubiously. What sort of platonic arrangement did he have in mind? In the same bed 'platonic' or in different rooms 'platonic'? Her belly curled at the thought. Did he *really* know the meaning of the word?

Visions of sharing the bed with him invaded her consciousness, taunting her body as to how close she'd be to his perfect body, how easy it would be to touch, taste and kiss him. Again?

'Cass.'

'What?' she snapped. Heat flooded her cheeks and she had to look away. If Matt guessed what had been going on in her mind she'd just die. She stared at the arrangement of the sitting room. 'You take the bed, I'll take the sofa.'

'I assumed that would be the case.' Matt yanked his shirt from the confines of his black trousers.

She didn't know what she'd expected, but she hadn't expected such easy compliance to her taking the short straw. She knew he'd been a bit in short supply of the 'gentleman' gene from the start… She took a breath. 'Fine.'

Cassie stomped into the sitting-room area. Sure, she was the stowaway, an interloper, homeless, but that didn't mean he could forget to be courteous. She was also a victim. And his guest, however unwelcome. She stared at the short lemon vinyl sofa and grimaced. She turned on her heel and stomped back. 'I need—' The words caught in her throat.

Matt had discarded his shirt. His bronzed shoulders, his muscular arms, his naked torso were all on exhibition. He looked up, threw her a pillow and yanked the bedspread off the bed and tossed it at her. 'Is that all?'

'Yes. Night.' She stomped back. How dared he know what she needed? How dare he take his shirt off while she was just metres away? He knew how she felt about last night. The last thing she needed was for him to flaunt his body in front of her, showing the bronzed expanse of flesh she'd already known intimately.

He was incorrigible.

She threw the pillow and cover on the sofa. It looked dubiously short but she figured that she'd have a better chance at sleep than Matt would have had, *if* he'd been a gentleman.

Cassie moved into a corner of the lounge where she knew Matt couldn't see her from the bedroom and unzipped her black gown. She wrapped the bedspread tightly around her. She'd be damned if she'd go and get her sleepwear from the drawer next to his bed. It was just tough for him if he got up early and found her sprawled half naked on the sofa. The vision popped into her mind—not much different from that of this morning.

She hesitated. Turned on her heel and stomped into his room. He was sprawled on the bed, his hands casually tucked behind his head. He only wore boxers, his long legs as muscular and appealing as the rest of him. Her mind taunted her with the pleasures of touch.

He glanced towards her. 'What now?'

'I need something to sleep in, if you don't mind.' Cassie moved to the drawer where she'd put her clothes earlier. She didn't miss the way his gaze careered over her. His mind probably making more of a fuss of her state than reality deemed necessary. There was no way on this planet that she'd end up in bed with him again!

'Fine.' He closed his eyes. 'Get it and get out. I need sleep. Some people are working tomorrow.'

She bristled. 'Other people would be too if some people hadn't got them blind drunk and made love to them all night.'

He opened his eyes, turned towards her and propped himself up on an elbow. 'We made love *all* night?'

'Didn't we? I mean…wouldn't we have?' The temperature rose in the room. She had to get away from this guy, and fast! She yanked open the drawer, holding her coverings tightly to her as she rummaged.

Matt smiled and leant back on the pillows and put his hands behind his head again. He stared at the ceiling. 'Probably. Hmm. Yes. All night.' His eyes roamed over her again. 'Yes, you'd probably be an all-nighter.'

She stared him in the face. His dark eyes gleamed with a promise that curled her toes and sent a rush of heat to the pit of her stomach. 'Maybe next time, you might not drink quite so much,' she accused. 'That way you might remember.'

'*Next* time?' Matt's voice was deep and husky.

She swallowed hard and plucked out her nightie. 'I meant the next woman.' Gawd, she was digging a hole for herself!

'*O-kay.* If you say so.'

Cassie turned and would have run to the sitting room if decorum, or the bedspread, had allowed. She snuggled in her private corner and slipped on the nightie. Damn the man for making her so mixed up she was left with both feet in her mouth!

She crawled onto the sofa and snuggled into the cushions and curled herself into a ball. She listened to the pounding of her heart and willed the ache inside to leave, quickly. She tried to think of Sebastian but visions of Matt invaded her mind. She was painfully aware he was only metres away.

*   *   *

Matt lay still, listening for her.

The moonlight shone in through the windows, where she lay, giving Matt enough light to examine the ceiling texture in great detail.

His chest ached, his guts ached and his mind was riddled with guilt. He should have let her have his bed. Heck, after what he'd done he should let her use his body to wipe her feet on. But she was just so damn irritating.

She seemed to get to him, like an itch that had to be scratched. He turned over, dragging the blanket with him. The pleasure and the pain in the scratching didn't escape him.

He tossed again. He couldn't get comfortable. She'd slept in this bed last night. He could almost distinguish her scent on the pillow.

Matt threw back the sheets and got up.

He ran a hand through his hair and paced the small room. The weight of his lies sat heavily in the pit of his gut. Torturing him. Reminding him of what he'd inflicted on Cass. What he had to make up for. She had enough troubles on her plate without him adding to them. Somehow, he had to convince her to dump Sebastian before she got hurt.

He lounged casually against the door frame, looking into the sitting room, watching her. The moonlight shone in through the window casting shadows over her face. She was beautiful.

He stroked his chin and took every detail in.

Everything about her taunted him. The way she was draped on the sofa, the shape of her full breasts, the creamy skin of her arm dangling off the makeshift bed, almost touching the floor. Even the tilt of her chin, the soft gentleness of her mouth and the serenity of her face mocked him. And if she thought that whisper-thin nightie was any better than being naked she was mistaken.

What was he doing? Matt strode across the room, pushed the curtain aside and yanked the sliding door open, stepping out onto the balcony.

The cold air enveloped him, cooling his body. He took several deep breaths. If it were winter he'd probably have icicles in his lungs—the voyage across to New Zealand was only taken in the summer months because of the damned chilly weather conditions, and the state of the ocean.

'What are you doing?'

He jerked. Hell. His worst nightmare! Her soft voice was unmistakable. Matt filled his lungs with sobering air and turned.

Cass stood in the doorway, the thin fabric of her nightie moving in the breeze. Her nipples stood erect, her legs impossibly long and silky white, her eyes sleepy.

His pulse pounded—the need to kiss away her sleepiness almost too much to bear—but he held his ground. 'Are you awake?'

'Of course I am.' She wrapped her arms around herself, her words fogging on the air. 'I wouldn't be talking to you if I wasn't.'

Matt shrugged. 'I've met some sleepwalkers in my time.'

'What are you doing out here? It's freezing.'

'Couldn't sleep.' He turned and leant against the rail. Maybe she'd go away. He counted his breaths. Waiting. He couldn't take much more of the cold. He was freezing his toes off!

'I didn't realise you had your own balcony,' Cass murmured, almost to herself.

Matt glanced at the pieces of furniture arranged there. A set of chairs snuggled in an intimate setting for two for breakfast, with a small round table in the middle and two deckchairs for sunbathing. 'Looks like it.'

'Great,' Cass said easily. 'It'd be terrific for a private tan.'

Her voice was soft, casual even, as though they were in conversation in a crowded cafe, not half naked and alone in the middle of the night, with her suggesting she was going to strip naked and tan herself on *his* balcony!

The urge to take her in his arms was excruciating. To touch her lips with his, to wrap himself around her… God, this was torture. This was absolute torture. What in blazes had he done to deserve this?

'Are you coming to bed?'

His heart jolted. 'Is that an invitation?'

Cass's eyes widened. She turned on her heel, stepped through the glass door and slid the sliding door shut.

Matt managed a laugh. She was so easy to tease. And for some reason he just couldn't help himself. He liked to see her react to him, no matter how.

The catch clicked loudly in the still night.

Matt darted a look at her. Cass smiled and waved to him through the thick glass.

He strode to the door. She wouldn't have. Couldn't have. He glanced to each side of him. The balconies were designed for privacy, not for commuting. The distance between them was a little too far for Matt to even consider. 'You didn't?'

She nodded.

Matt took a breath and tried the door. Locked. Damn. He could see the laughter in her eyes despite an attempt at seriousness on her face. She couldn't mean it. Not really. 'Open the door,' he demanded.

She shook her head and glanced back toward the bedroom. He could almost see the satisfaction written on her face. Not only would she get the bed to herself but exact some sort of warped revenge on him.

He jiggled from foot to foot, the chill of the balcony beneath his feet penetrating into his system. 'You can't leave me out here.'

She nodded, the smile growing. She threw her arms up and gave him a big shrug and moved away from the door. She turned away from him and sauntered towards his bed.

Matt couldn't miss the exaggerated roll to her hips—nor did his body. His blood roiled, his mind pondered her lying where he'd been, just minutes ago. Would his scent haunt her dreams? He doubted it. 'I'll consider the sofa,' he pleaded.

She turned at the bedroom doorway, backed up to

the bed and flopped down on it with an exaggerated sigh.

'It's freezing.' He stared at her through the glass. 'You can't do this. Please. I'll catch my death.'

She stared at him, her face sobering. He couldn't miss the way she nibbled her bottom lip or the intensity in her face.

He rubbed his arms and groaned for good measure, putting on his best impersonation of puppy-eyes.

She shook her head as she strode over to the door and unlocked it. 'Okay. So I don't want to be responsible for you getting sick.' She gave him a black look. 'Besides, I'd probably be lumped with looking after you. You men are such babies.'

'Are we?' He gritted his teeth and stepped into the cabin. He had half a mind to wipe her smile off her face with his lips, or toss her over his knee. Both ideas stirred his blood again.

Matt stood inches from her, fighting himself.

Cass stepped backwards.

He swallowed hard and strode into his bedroom.

'Where do you think you're going?' Her voice was pitched.

He flung the covers wide and slipped between them, willing the warmth back in his body. 'There's no way I'm sleeping on the sofa. But I'm willing to compromise since you showed me mercy. You're welcome to join me.'

He could hear her mutter some very unsavoury phrases. He smiled. There was no way she could beat him, that only left joining him. He tucked the blanket tightly around himself. He couldn't wait.

CHAPTER NINE

CASSIE wriggled deeper into the covers and massaged her neck muscles. She should have left Matt outside last night. If she had, she would have had a warm bed all to herself without any cricks at all. She rocked her head from shoulder to shoulder. The sofa was a kinker all right.

She glanced at her wrist. Her watch illuminated the time—six thirty-five a.m. She stared up at the ceiling. Only one night to go. And she was doing fine. Half the nightmare was over. She'd find ways to avoid Matt Keegan during the day and, at night, she'd focus on Sebastian, on the beautiful wedding she'd always wanted, and she'd pray.

She heard Matt stir.

Cassie pulled the covers up, over her face. There was no way she wanted to face any conversation about anything with him, especially her failed attempt at vengeance. She wished she could have seen it through, though—he deserved a night in the cold.

She slapped the cover down again. Her problem was that she was too nice. She needed to be mean, cruel and merciless. But seeing him shivering in the cold had hit her deeply in her chest. No matter what he'd done, she couldn't have let him suffer a whole night out on the balcony.

Cassie wasn't stupid either. She was vividly aware that the sun would rise and she'd have to face the music. And she was sure she wouldn't have wanted to be around for Matt's response to being frozen all night! She shook her head. Revenge wasn't her thing. It didn't come naturally. Maybe with a little practice. Maybe tonight…

She heard Matt pause in the doorway. Cassie could feel him watching her and her blood rushed through her system, her heart pounding. It was all she could do to keep her breathing deep and slow and her eyelids relaxed.

She'd used to fake being asleep when she was a child—but this was different. She fought the smile that threatened to break her façade. She wasn't ready for another bout with Matt just yet.

He moved away and she heard the bathroom door, then the shower. Visions of him standing there naked in all his bronzed glory invaded her mind.

She flung herself off the sofa.

This was her chance. She had to get dressed. Now. She'd rather do it while he was busy elsewhere than contemplate him bursting in on her. Finding her half naked. Seeing her body again.

She went to the drawer next to his rumpled bed where her clothes were. She couldn't help but glance at the indentation his head had made on the pillow, the way the other pillow was scrunched and mis-shapen as though he'd used it for boxing practice.

She pulled her attention away from the bed and plucked out what she needed from her drawer and quietly closed it. The shower had stopped. She willed her feet to move. She didn't want him to stare at her again with his deep, dark eyes, as he had last night on the balcony. It made her feel naked and vulnerable.

She slipped on her jeans and white vest-top in record time, but she fumbled with the white windcheater, conscious of the passing seconds. Cassie yanked it over her head and thrust her arms into the sleeves.

The bathroom door opened and Matt stepped out. A cream polo shirt hugged his oh-so-to-die-for chest, a pair of blue jeans fitted snugly on his narrow hips and long legs. His hair was wet, combed back, his face clean-shaven, his gaze intent as it roamed over her.

Her body reacted instantly. Her every nerve filled with a wanting that Cassie knew she was *not* going to answer. Not again, anyhow.

She grasped onto a thought. If she kept Sebastian firmly in her mind she'd be able to stay focussed, alert, and clear-headed.

'You're up.' His voice was soft and deep.

'Jeez, guys are so into stating the obvious,' Cassie blurted. She picked up the bedspread and pillow she'd used on the sofa, willing the surge of heat in her body to subside.

He raised his eyebrows. 'And good morning to you, too.'

'I would have a better one if it didn't include you.' She strode past him and tossed the bedding onto his bed. There was no way she was going to be nice—

ever! Last night's weakness wasn't going to happen again. He *did* deserve freezing all night.

'A bit harsh. Didn't you sleep well?'

The amusement in his voice was unmistakable. She opened her mouth, her eyes narrowing. Several choice expressions came to mind...

A knock on the door startled her.

'That's breakfast.' He strode to the door and opened it, casting her a knowing look.

Cassie clenched her teeth. He was so damn arrogant, so irritating, so annoyingly handsome.

A steward came in carrying a tray laden with pastries and fruit. 'Good morning. I hope you slept well.'

Cassie breathed in the sweet scent of croissants and coffee scrolls as the man moved past her to place the tray on the small occasional table.

'As well as could be expected.' She shot Matt her best attempt at an evil eye, hoping he got the message loud and clear. Maybe she should inform him how gentlemen were meant to behave!

The steward smiled and retrieved another tray from his cart in the hallway, oblivious to the tension between them.

Cassie leant towards the man, staring at the cups, saucers, milk and pots on his tray, the rich aroma seducing her senses. 'Coffee...'

'Yes, miss.'

Cassie didn't wait for the guy to even put the tray down. She grabbed an empty cup. Coffee was what she needed to get her mind back in order. She was suffering withdrawals, that was all. Matt's body wasn't *really* that crash hot.

'I'll leave you to it,' the uniformed guy said cheerily and headed for the door.

'Thank you,' Cassie sang as he closed the door. She poured the thick dark brew into her cup, dragging the rich scent in. Milk. Sugar. She lifted the cup and noticed Matt, leaning against the door frame, his thumb on his lips, stifling a smile. 'What?'

'Nothing. Just nice to see you so enthusiastic. Even if it's just a cuppa.'

'Just a cuppa?' She took a sip. Heaven. 'Bite your tongue.' But she couldn't help smiling. Having her routine wake-up coffee made a difference—it supported the idea that life did go on after Matt Keegan.

Matt laughed.

It sent ripples of pleasure radiating out from her stomach to her toes. She raised an eyebrow at him, shooting him a look of disdain. She didn't like Matt laughing at her.

He moved suddenly and reduced the distance between them. 'Want to make me one?'

Her heart beat a little faster. She stared into her coffee. It was the coffee, not him. 'I don't think you deserve one.'

He sat down beside her on the sofa, making it feel even shorter than it had felt last night. 'I'm paying for it.'

For the food or for what he'd done? She pursed her lips. 'Okay. When you put it that way.' But she moved down the sofa until she could feel the arm pushing hard against her thigh.

He sat back, watching her. A smile tugged at his mouth and his deep dark eyes glimmered suggestively. 'Milk, three sugars.'

Cassie dropped her attention to the task at hand. It was safer not to look at him, or suppose what was going through his mind. She poured him a coffee. 'Need the sweetness, do you?'

'What do you think?'

She pushed the sugar bowl towards him. 'I don't think there's enough sugar on the ship.' She nibbled the soft skin inside her cheek. Would he bite back?

Matt added the sugar, stirred the brew and took the coffee. 'What are you planning to do today?'

Cassie let go of the breath she was holding. 'No idea. I think I'm going to be bored senseless.' Why wasn't he rising to her bait? Wasn't she worth it?

He sat up and took a gulp of his drink. 'There's plenty of on-board activities.'

'Which I've neither paid for nor am entitled to.' She drank some more of her coffee. Never again would she be caught like this. As soon as she got home she'd see to having her credit card stapled to her butt. Anything other than feel like a freeloading stowaway!

Matt shrugged. 'You're my guest now, so you can do whatever you like.'

She shook her head. 'No. I can't. And I won't.' She wasn't going to pretend this was all okay.

'Fine.' He drew his lips in thoughtfully. 'Well, I guess you could catch up on some more reading in the library. That wouldn't be like you'd be flat-out enjoying yourself.'

Cassie cringed at the thought of trying to focus on another book when her life was crumbling around her. She took another sip and put her cup down on the table.

Matt smiled. 'I'm sure you'll find something to do that'll keep you busy.' He snatched up the coffee scroll and slapped some butter on it. He stood up.

'I guess I'll manage.' She wasn't repelled by the idea of hiding in the cabin the whole day—that way she wouldn't have to face anyone or risk running into Matt. Her gaze strolled up his long denim-clad legs, over his slim hips and up his wide chest.

Matt bit down on his scroll. 'Well, have a lovely day. Just don't get in my way, okay.' He strode to the door.

She raised her hands. That was more like him. 'Fine by me.'

Cassie watched the door close. She collapsed back onto the sofa and sighed. Thank goodness that was over. She'd survived. But she hadn't thought of Sebastian at all!

Later that morning Matt strode along the Sunkissed Deck scanning the bodies browning in the mid-morning sunshine. She was here somewhere. And when he got his hands on her...he had absolutely no idea what he'd do with her.

She was getting to him. Burrowing her way through his defences with her gentleness, her softness, her gorgeous green eyes and sulky full lips. Even this morning had caught him off guard. He'd expected her to be repentant, not feisty and challenging. It was all he could do to hold his tongue and keep his distance.

Cass lay in the sun at the end of the deck. She'd discarded the windcheater and the jeans, laying bare her body to the elements. Trent had been one hundred per cent correct. She had said she was going to work on her tan *and* on schedules.

Matt dragged air into his lungs.

She was stretched out on the sun-lounger. Her toes were long, the nails varnished with a soft pink shade. He couldn't help but follow the line of her legs, up her calves, her knees, and up, to her soft ivory thighs.

She wore the white vest-top she'd modelled for him, her figure all curves, her hands full of papers, a pen balanced in the corner of her temptingly curved mouth. His eyes darted down again. The bikini pants she wore were impossibly small, covering very little of her.

Blood surged to his loins. 'What are you doing?' His voice came out harsh, accusing.

Cass didn't even flinch. 'I'm working.'

'At what, may I ask? Carl said he'd spoken to you.' He couldn't have her snooping around. She might just find out the truth and then any reasoning with her would be thrown overboard.

'Nothing that concerns you, yet.' Cass tossed him an innocent smile, her green eyes flashing.

Did she have any idea how she affected him? Matt darted a glance around the other patrons. She hadn't escaped the men's notice at all. 'Had many free drinks?'

She plucked the pencil out of her mouth and raised an eyebrow. 'How did you know? You're not turning psychic on me, are you?'

'You know, they come with strings attached.' Didn't she realise? His muscles clenched deep in his gut. He'd used the ploy himself a hundred times to justify an introduction. She could be inviting all sorts of weirdos to proposition her.

'And yours don't come with strings?' She raised her eyebrows at him and crossed her legs—the movement slow and exact.

His eyes were drawn again to her long bare legs. His blood heated and he shifted uncomfortably. 'Look, get up will you? Let's talk somewhere else.'

'Fine. Okay. But there's no need to get upset. I'm wearing sunscreen.' She swung her legs over the side of the lounger and stood up.

He was right. The bikini covered very little indeed.

'Where're your jeans?' He wanted to stand in front of her, behind her, cover her up so no one else feasted on the sight of her body.

'Right here.' She picked them up off the back of the chair. 'Is there a problem?'

'Damn right there is.' He gestured to her jeans in her hand. 'Put them on.'

She stood there for a moment. Her eyes had narrowed and he was sure she was going to fight him on this. He knew he was acting like her father but, damn it, she couldn't swan around the ship like this. Anything could happen.

Cass moved slowly. Placing one finely arched foot into the leg of the jeans, then the other. She shimmied the light denims up her hips slowly, rocking her body from side to side, catching his eyes with hers, the challenge apparent.

Matt ran a hand through his hair. 'Damn it, Cass. Did you take them off right here, like this?' Had she any idea what she was doing? What forces she was playing with? His body was desperate for her.

Her lips quivered, a smile pulling at the corners of her full mouth. She flipped the button on her jeans and yanked up the zip. 'No one else has a problem.'

He moved closer to her. 'What are you doing? This isn't you.'

He saw her start, the hurt in her eyes. She lowered her lashes. 'You have no idea what is or isn't me! You have no idea at all. You crash into my perfect life, make a God-awful mess and don't even remember my name!'

Matt opened his mouth. Then closed it. He couldn't just blurt out the truth. Not here. Not like this.

Cass looked around him to the far end of the deck. 'Have you seen Rob around?'

He sobered. 'Why?' An icy chill cooled his desire. She couldn't have guessed. Dread crept into his system at the notion she'd found out the truth on her own and he would never get a chance to explain.

'Okay, so I'll tell you,' she said lightly. She put a hand on her hip. 'I've already taken notes from Carl and Trent in their breaks and I'm forming some very interesting theories on how to manage their time more efficiently.'

She didn't know. He let out the breath he was holding.

He threw his shoulders back. 'Look, can we talk in the shade?' He didn't miss the dusty-rose flush on her cheeks, on her shoulders.

'Why?'

'You don't want to get too much sun.' And he didn't want these guys watching her.

'Next, you'll be volunteering to rub lotion on my back.'

His blood surged. He swallowed the lump of desire pulsing inside him. 'Maybe later.'

She darted him a look, then stalked to the shaded area beside the bar. The stools were full of people so she stopped in the walkway. 'So…do you want to hear about my ideas or not?'

Matt opened his mouth but the words escaped him. He was drowning in her green eyes, in the soft scents of her invading his senses, of her smooth, soft skin beckoning to him. He stiffened. He *wanted* her!

A group of people surged toward them, with drinks in their hands, towels and bags. They invaded what little space there was on their way to the pool.

Cass had to pick the main thoroughfare to stand! They were jostled. Matt grabbed her, pressing her warm body up against the wall, shielding her from harm.

Sensations sizzled into Cass's system. She wasn't

sure she liked the feeling at all. 'Let go of me.' She dragged herself out of his hold and clenched her hands stiffly at her sides.

This wasn't the idea. She'd decided work was the only thing to keep her mind off Matt Keegan and here he was, again.

'Sorry.' He took a deep, unsteady breath and stepped backward. He looked into her eyes.

There was a gentleness in his look that spoke directly to her body. Her heart pounded. It was becoming increasingly obvious how she succumbed to the man!

Cass sucked in a calming breath. She should have known that Matt wouldn't stay in the background while she quizzed the rest of the staff.

'Yes, well.' She stepped away from his tense, hard body and rubbed her fingertips over the wad of papers in her hand. 'I wasn't going to tell you until I'd worked it out. We could streamline several areas of your business, making your employees' time more cost-effective.'

'Really? That sounds interesting.' His eyes were sharp and assessing. 'What has this got to do with Rob?'

'I thought I'd talk to her about details. Carl said she was like your right-hand man, woman…?' Talking to Rob had seemed like the perfect opportunity to gather the information she needed to compile her report without getting in *his* way. Which was her main aim.

It was a great idea. It not only kept her busy but

also would reduce the debt she felt to Matt, for the money he'd spent on her. The sooner she paid that back in some way, the better she'd feel.

'Why not talk to me? I'm *the* hand.' His tone was soft, gentle with a quiet emphasis that suggested surprise at her decision to talk to Rob instead of him.

She frowned and shifted from foot to foot. There was no way she was going to admit the effect he had on her scared her to pieces. 'You said not to bother you.'

'I've changed my mind.' There was a lethal calmness in his eyes, in the soft tone of his voice.

'But you're so busy.' She licked her lips nervously. Why would he want to change his mind now? He'd been all for her keeping away from him this morning... 'I wouldn't want to take you away from your work.'

He shoved his hands into his pockets. 'I don't want you interrupting Rob. She's doing some very exact calculations and analysis, so stay away from her.'

'I was going to talk to her on her breaks.' She tilted her chin up and glared him in the eye. Talk about a protective boss. And what was the deal with dragging her out of the sun and demanding she get dressed? This guy was having delusions of power, big time. She was just glad she could reciprocate by pushing his buttons.

'No. Talk to *me*.' His dark eyes didn't leave hers for an instant. 'At lunch. I'll meet you up on the Sunrise Deck at one.'

'But Rob—' She wanted Robyn's view on the company and its inefficiencies, not his. She definitely didn't want to spend any more time with *him*.

'Forget about Rob.' His dark eyes pierced her with a demand for compliance. 'She's busy. Leave her alone. Okay?'

Cassie waved the papers between them to ward off his intensity. 'Okay.' She managed a shrug. 'Sunrise Deck at one.'

She watched Matt turn and admired the way his butt moved as he sauntered off. He did have a cute behind in blue jeans.

She shook herself, the reality of the situation seeping into her mind. It was just what she didn't want. Serious alone time with Matt Keegan. Matt's complete and undivided attention.

Maybe she could wriggle out of the idea. It was stupid in the first place. Why work when she could laze in the sun on this gorgeous liner with nothing but her thoughts for company? Thinking about Sebastian, her wedding and what a mess she'd made of everything. Spending time with her guilt would be far better than spending time with Matt.

Cassie bit down on her fingernail. She'd have to make some excuse, something brilliant. She'd got out of awkward appointments before. She didn't see any reason why Matt would be any different. He wouldn't care anyway. It wasn't as if he were really interested.

'Oh, and Cass.' Matt turned back. 'It sounds like a great idea, something our company would appreciate the help with.' And he strode off.

Cassie stamped her foot. Damn. How could she get out of it now?

CHAPTER TEN

IT DIDN'T take Cassie long to figure out that the Sunrise deck didn't have a restaurant. Matt could have mentioned the fact when he'd invited her to eat there. Where, she had no idea. There wasn't much to it. A jogging track ran around the perimeter, with a raised platform in the middle complete with its own railing, designed specifically, she guessed, for observing the glorious vista of sunrises and sunsets on the ship.

Cassie leant on the rail and watched a couple of joggers do the circuit. There was a very quiet, relaxed mood on the almost deserted deck. The place wasn't exactly a happening venue…

She stared out at the expanse of water around her, spreading to every horizon like patterned blue glass. It was overwhelming. She felt very small. Very far away from her life in Sydney.

Her watch blinked reassuringly at her—twelve fifty-eight p.m.

Cassie pushed herself away from the rail and walked slowly along the deck. She wasn't in any hurry to meet Matt Keegan. She had an inkling that there was more going on with the guy than a cute face, great body and a womanising attitude. And she wasn't sure whether she'd be able to handle whatever he was planning on throwing at her next.

Four more days to her wedding. She had to hang onto that fact and Sebastian. Tension rose in her stomach. She closed her eyes. Everything had to go to plan on Saturday.

She needed this wedding more than anything. She needed to have some semblance of normality again. She needed someone to hold her safe at night. She needed to have a life without lies. Like the lie Tom had fed her to keep her with him, while he'd enjoyed another woman's bed. Like the lies her parents had perpetrated on her, pretending life had all been okay when it hadn't been.

The deck was enormous. Cassie walked slowly. A figure was on the far end of the deck.

Her heart skipped. It was Matt. He was already there, sitting on a red checked rug with a basket beside him looking for all the world as if he had nothing better to do than wait for her. He faced the front of the ship looking toward the horizon.

She walked toward him, her nerves jangling and alarm bells ringing somewhere deep in her mind. She couldn't put her finger on it, but she knew the game plan had changed. And she was in trouble.

The blanket was decked out for a romantic interlude. She didn't miss the connotation in the intimate settings; the two-of-everything-type look, meticulously arranged. The two wineglasses, the flower next to the plate she'd be sitting at, the closeness of the settings themselves.

Matt turned. 'Hi, Cass.' His voice caressed her name. 'Like it?'

'No. You're scaring me.' She rubbed her hands down her jeans in an effort to dispel the tingling sensation in them.

'What do you mean? *This.*' He gestured to the picnic. 'It's nothing.' He shook his head, his voice casual and undemanding. 'I just want to apologise. Truly. For that first night. And for last night. I've been a heel.'

'No.' Cassie stepped back. 'Don't do this.' Her hands twisted together, rubbing her skin, grinding the muscles.

The beginning of a smile tipped the corners of his mouth. 'What? I'm not doing anything.' He tried to look innocent. 'Didn't you want me to apologise?' His eyes were compelling, magnetic.

She did. She had. Desperately. She wanted him to know she was a person with feelings, with a heart, with a life. She swallowed. Maybe she was too convincing. 'Ye-e-s.' She was tentative.

'Then—' he gestured to the rug and the placing opposite him for her to sit down '—you're not *really* scared, are you?'

She knew his words for what they were. A challenge. A ploy to get her to accept, but despite the knowledge she couldn't bring herself to walk away. Something deep inside her told her she had to see this through. No matter what.

Cassie sat on the rug and met Matt's gaze. She

managed a choking laugh. 'So what's all this niceness in aid of?'

His eyes flashed with innocence. 'Can't I be nice, just because I am?'

She moistened her dry lips. 'Likely story. From the moment I first met you I haven't made any sense out of you or this…' she spread her arms wide '…this situation.'

'And from the moment I met you—' his eyes bored into hers '—I've been surprised, confronted and confounded.' He sucked in a breath. 'Can we call a truce?' He thrust out his hand.

She eyed it dubiously. His hands looked as strong as they looked persuasive, if only she remembered. She shook herself. It was good she couldn't remember that first night with him. Matt Keegan looked to be an unforgettable experience, a night that could have shadowed her relationship with Sebastian for ever more, if she remembered…

Sebastian.

She darted a glance to where his engagement ring sometimes sat. The diamond ring might not be there. But her commitment was. Wasn't it? So, she wasn't exactly thinking of him much…but there were extenuating circumstances. Like Matt.

It wasn't as if she was comparing them. There was nothing to compare. Sebastian was tall. Matt was taller. Sebastian was light-framed, Matt generously muscled. Sebastian was cool, calm and collected at all times. Matt was unpredictable, surprising. Sebastian was safe. Matt was…out of the question.

Matt dropped his hand with a slight shrug. 'Wine?' Matt lifted the wine bottle to the mouth of her glass and the deep red vintage streamed out. 'I thought we could talk.'

Cassie knew that wasn't a good idea. Sure, there was heaps she wanted to know about him, questions that were taunting her mind, fuelling her curiosity about him. But there was a certain amount of safety in ignorance, in unfamiliarity. And as far as she was concerned, she'd already been far too familiar with this guy.

'So, you have a cat called Frizzle and you live in Sydney just like me.'

She frowned at him. 'I don't remember telling you I live in Sydney.' She was sure she hadn't and the fact that Matt could live in the same city as her, maybe the same suburb, was very disturbing. A rush of blood heated her entire body, and she shifted uncomfortably.

He looked at her blankly. 'You must have said, that first night. Sunday night.' And he looked out to sea again.

That was one subject she'd like to avoid. 'So, what are we eating?' She stared at the basket, willing him not to pursue that particular subject. She was feeling far too vulnerable to his deep voice and warm smile for *that* conversation.

Any recounting of Sunday night's events, in all their sensual detail, would be her undoing. It was hard enough to keep her fantasies of what they'd done at bay as it was.

Matt ignored the basket. 'You have two brothers?'

'Yes.' She stared into his dark eyes, glad that he'd let her change the subject. She clenched her hands tightly on her lap. He was *serious* about 'talking'. And the fact was scarier than his secrets. 'And you only have Rob—' She stared at the setting in front of her, hoping he took the hint without feeling obliged to tell her anything.

Matt stared into his wine and then out to sea.

Cassie figured he was priming himself for another escape, from revealing his past to her. She shifted restlessly, but didn't take her eyes off him. Maybe she wanted him to go and not share any more of his life with her...

'He was six years younger than me.' He ran a hand through his hair. 'The gate had been left open to the pool.' He swallowed hard. 'Someone...found him and got him out...but it was too late.'

'I'm sorry.' She couldn't imagine how hard it would be to lose someone close like that. Didn't want to. How it must have affected him. She lay her hand over his on the rug. She didn't know what else to do.

'I suppose I just want to keep Rob safe.' His voice broke and he snapped his attention out to sea again.

Cassie sat still. She wanted to hold him in her arms and tell him he'd done a great job—she'd turned out okay—but she was frozen to the spot. She was a stranger. One that had shared the night with him, was sharing this personal moment with him, but that was all.

Her heart warmed at the connection. He was showing her the real Matt Keegan. And by heavens, he was looking fine from where she sat.

'Anyway.' He cleared his throat and covered her hand with his other one, encapsulating hers in his warmth. 'I guess I just wanted you to know. Know where I'm coming from.'

A shiver rippled through her at his touch. 'But where are you heading?' She bit her tongue. She wasn't inviting herself into his life. She already had one. A very organised, efficient one all mapped out and ready to go. Cassie pulled back her hand, still tingling.

Matt pierced her with his dark probing eyes. 'You don't have to marry him.'

Cassie started. 'What?'

'How do you know he's the one for you?' His voice deepened, his tone husky—it held a challenge.

She took a sip of wine, casting a longing glance out to sea. She had to focus. On Sebastian. Sebastian, her rock. Sebastian, the ordered and efficient. Sebastian, the perfect and prompt.

'If you knew him you'd see he's perfect for me. He's gentle, well mannered…' She glanced back at Matt, trying to ignore the fact that she was stuck for words. 'He respects my job, my ambitions. We like the same things. We like the same suburbs. Same political views.'

'Sounds boring. Are you sure you're not carrying a bit of emotional baggage that colours your vision where he's concerned?'

'No!' How dared he even presume to think along

the lines of her emotional issues? 'And our relationship is not boring. Neither is Sebastian.' Her face
heated. 'Who are you to throw criticisms around, anyway? You're the one that slept with a drunken woman
without even knowing her name.'

'*Touché.*' Matt took salad and cold meats out of
his basket, placing them on the plates. 'But, as a
friend, it sounds like you've picked yourself a very
efficient, inexpensive item of furniture, or a pet.'

'You're mistaken. I'm very much in…in—' She
looked down at her plate, then up again, meeting his
dark eyes. 'In…volved.'

'Right. Okay.'

She could hear the mockery in his tone. She might
not be able to say *I love you* to anyone, but that didn't
mean she didn't. Since her parents' divorce she just
couldn't make herself say those words. 'You probably
think you're so smart.' She put down her glass.

'I have a diploma to prove it.' His dark eyes
gleamed with insolence.

'Is that all?' she scoffed. She leant closer to him,
jutting out her chin in defiance.

'And a degree.' He challenged her, his face centi-
metres from her own, the corners of his mouth threatening to break into one of his devastating smiles.

'No doctorate?' She laughed, breathing in his
sweet, tangy cologne. She couldn't help but notice the
scent was mingled intoxicatingly with pure, gorgeous
male.

'No, no doctorate.' His mouth twitched. 'But what
have you got?'

She hesitated only a moment. She'd show him what she damn well had!

She brushed her mouth against his.

His lips were as warm as she'd imagined. Soft too. He was motionless for only a second, then his danced to life beneath hers, sending frissons of awareness jolting through her system.

Matt's kiss was gentle, persuasive, and intoxicating. The sweet exploration of his mouth dominated Cassie's senses. Every nerve buzzed, every hair stood on end, and every part of her was drowning in the havoc his kiss evoked within her.

Sensation thrummed through her.

Her hands itched to explore the perfection of his body, feel the hard muscles beneath her fingertips, stroke the length of his back and call up the power that she knew lay coiled within him, carefully hidden under layers of control.

She couldn't miss the heat emanating from his body, the soft touch of his hand brushing her hair from her face, how his thumb tenderly traced the line of her cheekbone and jaw, how his body beckoned to hers.

Matt pulled back, leaving her lips burning with fire.

'Why did you do that?' he murmured, his eyes blazing down into hers. 'Not that I mind or anything, but I was just wondering.'

Cassie sobered, her stomach lurching. 'I didn't. You did.'

Matt shook his head, staring at her lips as though he was considering more of the same.

Cassie moistened her lips. '*I* did?' She touched her own chest vaguely, reality setting in. She had! And all she wanted was to do it again. She'd never tasted anyone as sweet, had lips so sensual roaming over her own, experienced anything quite like Matt Keegan before in her life. And she had no idea whether that was a good thing…or not.

CHAPTER ELEVEN

CASSIE'S heart pounded in her chest. Her lips tingled. It was all she could do to maintain a façade of calm. *That kiss.* She picked at the salad on her plate, her cheeks burning at her stupidity. She had willingly and soberly kissed Matt Keegan!

She piled a load of salad on her fork and stared morosely at it. What was she going to do now? What the hell could she say to get herself out of this mess?

Focussing on the food did little to solve her dilemma.

The strained silence between them threatened Cassie with indigestion. She wanted to break it. Say something that could clear the air, and dampen the energy that sizzled between them.

She had no idea why she'd done it. Probably some remnant of his charms on her drunken mind the first night. And she regretted it. Not how it had felt. But that she'd felt it, so sweetly, so thoroughly, and so deeply. She had some idea now of what her mind must be suppressing deep in her subconscious and she was glad it was.

Cassie took another mouthful of salad. She was confused, that was all. How did she let herself be affected by Matt, of all people? You'd think she would've learnt by now.

Her mind darted back to her childhood, and that valentine boy. She couldn't even remember his name any more but the hurt was still with her. It wasn't enough that he'd played a joke on her—to share it with the rest of the form had been despicable. As Tom was despicable.

Tom, she wasn't going to forget easily. She'd weathered her parents' surprise divorce with him by her side. She'd grown out of the awkwardness, the puppy fat, but not the luck she had with boys. Or lack of.

Tom had been her first love. At nineteen she'd been on top of the world, she'd had the guy she loved at her side, and life had been looking up again after her parents' divorce. Her parents' separation hadn't affected her. Not really. Not with Tom there to love her.

When she'd arrived home from university early and found him in the arms of another woman it had hurt, deeply. She'd thought everything had been fine, everything had been perfect—and it hadn't been. Painfully, embarrassingly, hadn't been.

It had taken her several chocolate binges, a ton of affirmations, six movie-marathons and a haircut to get over him. Five years ago. She shook her head. Time flew. But she was over him. There was no way she was carrying the baggage that Matt had accused her of.

She stared out over the water, avoiding looking in Matt's direction. She should have known better than to kiss Matt. She wasn't stupid. She prided herself on her intelligence. She touched her still-tingling lips to the side of her wineglass and took a gulp of the rich red wine.

'I'm getting married on Saturday,' she blurted. 'And there's nothing you can say to dissuade me, even if I wanted to be dissuaded, which I definitely do not!'

Matt looked up and raised his eyebrows. 'Then what was that kiss about?'

His voice was deep and husky, resonating through her, reminding every nerve in her body of her attraction to him. She clenched her teeth. 'It meant nothing.'

He fixed her with his golden-flecked dark eyes. 'It didn't feel like nothing.'

The space on the deck suddenly shrank. She wriggled backwards on the rug, feigning a more comfortable position, gaining precious distance between them. 'It did from where I was sitting.'

Matt put down his fork and wiped his mouth with a napkin. 'And that was from the kisser's standpoint?'

She shrugged. 'So we're getting all picky about who's the kisser and who's the kissee now, are we?' She gulped some more wine. She didn't want to even begin to find a reasonable excuse for the kiss. 'Then what did *you* think?'

'About the kiss?' His eyes smiled at her, his tongue flicking over his lips.

She cringed. Why did she ask? She had to have some masochistic tendency. She held her breath. If he felt anything the way she did...

Matt shrugged. 'It was…nice.'

She expelled her breath. She didn't know what she'd been expecting, but not that. 'That was all?' Her voice rose in pitch. 'Nice?' She licked her lips and narrowed her eyes at him.

Matt looked up at the puffy white clouds hanging overhead. 'I'm having trouble describing the sensation.'

'Really?' She gritted her teeth. 'Try.'

'Soft, warm—' He clicked his fingers as though the motion would help him choose the right word. His mouth curved into an unconscious smile.

'Riveting, sensational, stirring?' she offered, her eyes wide, her blood starting to heat at his casual indifference. Why did she even consider that this guy was worth a second thought?

'Hmm…' Matt shot her an irresistibly devastating grin. 'Yep, the world moved for me, too.'

'The world did not move for me!' She shook her head. Great. She couldn't keep her mouth shut, could she? She filled it with a lettuce leaf. If she kept the damn thing full she couldn't trip over her own tongue.

Matt shrugged dismissively. 'Now, about your plans for my business.'

'Plans?' She jerked. 'Yes. Of course.' Safe ground. He was letting her back out of her terrible mistake of kissing him. There *was* some saving quality about him.

Matt glanced at his watch. 'Is that the time? I have to get back to work, but how about we talk later, at dinner, about what you have in mind?' He put the dishes back into the picnic basket.

Cassie snatched her bread roll as he yanked her plate away and stowed it in the basket. He certainly wasn't wasting any time about packing up.

'We were meant to talk now.' She stood up and watched him fold the blanket and place it on top of the basket. She didn't exactly want another opportunity to look an idiot in front of him.

Matt straightened, fixing her with an assessing look. 'Well, we didn't quite get around to that did we?' He rested his gaze on her lips.

Her body tingled in response. Damn it. 'No, we didn't.'

'So, have all your notes handy. We'll get into it tonight.' He bent down and picked up the basket.

Cassie's eyes were drawn involuntarily to how well he filled his denims. His butt looked so good in those tight jeans.

He turned.

She smoothed some imaginary wrinkles out of her jeans, examining them closely, willing her cheeks not to heat. 'No worries.'

'Okay. I'll organise everything.' Matt hardly gave her a glance. He turned and strode off.

Cassie willed her feet to follow. There didn't seem much to arrange if they were dining with his team again. She almost could look forward to spending some time with his sister—maybe she'd be a willing shoulder to cry on? 'Exactly what are you organising?' she called after him.

He turned. 'Dinner in our cabin, of course,' he said casually. 'We need somewhere quiet to go over your assessment and recommendations. What better place than the solitude of our cabin?'

Our cabin? What happened to the 'his'? Her courage sank to her toes. 'Yes,' she said vaguely. Her mind whirled at the possible connotations, and her tongue seemed to stick to the roof of her mouth. 'See you.'

Matt's stride was long, almost a swagger as he left her behind. Standing still. Cassie bit hard down on her bottom lip.

There was no way she could avoid him. Short of jumping off the boat she'd have to go back to his cabin some time, and face the music, knowing the world had moved for him...

He wouldn't take the kiss the wrong way. It was a mistake. He knew that. Had to. She was almost a married woman.

Cassie frowned. What had she started?

Cassie felt her lips; his kiss still burned in her mind. Why she'd let herself be carried away by the moment eluded her. It wasn't as though she even liked the guy.

She leant back into a lounge chair in the bar area, watching the couples passing her. The holding hands, the soft looks, the gentle words—her gut ached. She wanted it all, so much.

Sebastian was proper. He refused to hold hands in public, touch her except in the most impersonal way, and his words were saved more for his voters than for her.

She sighed. But he made sense. He was wealthy, with a career, with the same interests. So he was a bit repressed. She could teach him otherwise.

They could work out how to make her feel that glorious pull from deep inside when he kissed her, the delightful shivers down her spine when he touched her, the excitement that bubbled up inside her from just a look, a laugh. They could work it out.

She rubbed her hand over her eyes.

So Matt Keegan evoked sensations in her that she'd never felt before. That didn't give him a monopoly on the effect. Sebastian could do it for her, too. If they worked out how.

She watched a young couple walk in, their hands entwined, their bodies touching, their steps in rhythm with each other. There was no hesitation on where to sit. No struggle to get comfortable. They entangled themselves in each other's arms as they sat and started kissing. Deep, passionate, dreamy kisses that made Cassie ache for Matt's lips.

She sighed. Who was she kidding? Matt had a way about him that called to something primal in her. Something that she might never find with Sebastian. Or anyone else.

So she'd have to assess what was more important to her, that was all. She had her mind, her logic and it could help her out of this little dilemma as efficiently and as effectively as any other problem she'd been faced with.

So what if Matt made her *feel*? Her heart wasn't the issue. Logic was superior. Always had been. Always would be. She'd relied on it when her parents had split up, when Tom had cheated on her *and* when she'd met Sebastian. Trusting her heart led to pain and anguish, and logic was safe and sure.

The couple laughed together, sharing their drinks and food with each other as though it was the most natural thing in the world.

Cassie could see herself and Matt just like that, wrapped in each other, sharing, giving, tasting all life had to offer together. A warm glow caressed her deep in her chest.

She felt empty. Alone. Her eyes burned and she had to look away.

She straightened. What Matt offered, she had no idea. She'd spent a long time trusting her logic. But there was no way she wanted to spend a lifetime re-gretting not taking this opportunity. She was older now. It was time to take one last try at trusting her heart. And if this attraction to Matt was something special, that it could grow to something akin to love, she owed it to herself to give it a chance.

Cassie crossed her fingers. She would see where her heart took her and, hopefully, she'd survive the experience.

CHAPTER TWELVE

MATT KEEGAN rolled his shoulders in an effort to release some of the tension as he walked down the corridors of the ship to his cabin. His neck was stiff, his body tense. The rest of the day had gone well and the job was working out fine, but he wished he could say the same about Cassie.

That kiss!

She'd taken him by surprise. And the surprise couldn't have been a nicer, warmer, more moving one. Her lips had been magical, everything he'd imagined them to be, and more.

The fact that she'd felt the same energy as he had, that charge, that need, touched him deep inside. And the sensation was more pleasant, more comfortable, and more addictive than he could ever have imagined.

He balled his fists. He wasn't going to let her be hurt. There was no way Sebastian was going to get away with this.

Matt wanted everyone to find out what a heartless, ladder-climbing creep Sebastian was. How low this man would go. Fancy blackmailing him to convince his fiancée that she'd compromised herself and their relationship so she'd break off the wedding.

He shuddered. There was no doubt that Sebastian saw his career as more important than Cass, and her feelings. But how could the guy set her up like this after knowing her, loving her, seeing what a lovely person she was?

Matt clenched his jaw. Sebastian was preying on the fact that his public would empathise with him being dumped. Poor Cass. She had no idea what mayhem she'd be walking back into when she arrived back in Australia.

Matt didn't buy Sebastian's innocence for one minute. *That* Eva woman was involved in this somehow. There was no other explanation for her zealous role in arranging Cassie in the bed, in the cabin. How? Matt had no idea. He didn't even want to think about it. Eva had probably drugged her…

He wanted to punch a wall. Fooling around on Cass was incomprehensible. Doing this to Cass was unbelievable. She was everything a man could want…everything he wanted.

Matt's stride faltered.

So he wanted her. There was nothing special in that. She was a damned pretty woman. It was natural. Nothing more. So she irritated the hell out of him, and had crept under his skin—it didn't mean anything.

He lengthened his stride. Sebastian's plan was ruthless, to say the least. His aim was to get Cass out of the picture so he could pursue his relationship with that other woman without damaging his precious public image. He was relying on the fact Cass would tell him what had happened. And by the sounds of it, she'd tell him, all right. Throw herself on his mercy and he'd heap on the guilt until he shone clean.

Matt slammed his fist into his other palm. Why was she making it so difficult? Why didn't she take the hint and leave the creep and start feeling instead of thinking?

He turned down a corridor. Because she didn't know.

He slowed his pace. It was up to him to warn her, show her in some way what was going on so she could make the right decision. And dump the creep without putting Rob at risk.

Cass was all but begging him to rescue her. With her eyes, with her touch, with her lips. He hesitated. But how much was she doing things because of what had supposedly happened between them rather than pure, unadulterated instinct?

He wanted to awaken that in her. He owed her that. It was something he knew how to do. His father had gone out of his way to show him the merits of following your heart.

His father had suffered for years in the suburbs denying his dreams because the family orchards had been left to his older brother, not him. It was only when he'd moved to his own hobby farm that he'd started really living, really smiling. Matt paused at the cabin door. He owed her that.

Matt opened the cabin door.

Papers were spread from one end of the sitting room to the other. Cass had to have drained the ship's supplies. She had them stacked and spread everywhere leaving only two areas clear. A square metre on the floor and a square metre on the sofa.

Matt didn't miss the significance. He dragged in a lungful of air. Maybe he was wrong about her wanting to be rescued. It looked as if he was going to have more work than he thought.

He moved to the sofa and sank into it, leaning his elbows heavily on his knees, staring down at the paper wall piled in front of him.

'Hi.' Cass stood at the balcony doorway. Her blue jeans still hugged her curvaceous legs and hips, the same windcheater he'd seen this morning covered her breasts, arms and stomach. Her hair neat, her eyes wary.

'I ordered a late dinner.' He looked at the paper between them. 'So we can concentrate on this. Is this all your proposal?' He damn well hoped he could get her to stop thinking about work for five minutes and confront the Sebastian issue.

She tilted her head to one side. 'Not really. Some of this is for other clients—from memory.' She looked sheepish. 'I had to do something or I'd have gone mad with boredom.' She pointed at the piles closest to the sofa. 'These ones are for your company.'

Her full lips mesmerised him as they moved, as did the rest of her body as she wove effortlessly around the piles to the square of vacant carpet in the middle of the room.

She sat on her own, surrounded by paper, keeping a safe distance between them. She was shutting him out. If she succeeded, he wouldn't get through to her. He needed to be close, break down her walls, sneak in his hints of Sebastian's treachery.

'It's not that complicated, really. I'll explain it.'

'Can you explain something else?' Matt took a breath. He had to do this. She was going home to-morrow. She had to guess the truth about Sebastian. 'How can you tell if you love someone?'

Cass's eyes widened and she stared at him.

He had her attention.

'I don't know.' She licked her lips. 'I guess, you feel special deep inside.'

A good guess. There was no way Sebastian could make her feel that. 'And what else?'

'He makes you wonder about where all the feelings have been. At just how much you can feel and how dull your life was before, I guess.'

Matt swallowed. She had to love Sebastian. It sounded like love to him. Or she could be referring to *him*. He felt a swell of warmth in his chest and an ache deep in the pit of his gut. He swallowed hard. He was being an idiot. Delusional! She couldn't mean *him*. 'And when he kisses you, touches you…?'

'You want to melt into him,' she said softly.

His gut lurched. 'And then you want to marry him?' As she wanted to marry Sebastian. The stupid fool. He really had her love and he was going to just throw it away.

She nodded. She moved to a pile of paper in front of her and picked it up. 'These are the notes for Trent's schedule.' She put it to one side and picked up the next pile in front of it. 'This is Carl's.' She picked it up and put it aside.

She fixed him with her gorgeous green eyes and he couldn't help the response pounding through his body. His heart thundered, his blood heated, his hands itched to reach out and touch her, his lips to kiss her.

'And this would be Rob's, if I knew it.' She picked up the pile. She shrugged at his glance to the pile. 'You told me I wasn't allowed to interrupt her, so I made some notes using Trent's and Carl's. I just need her to fill in the details.'

It wasn't Rob's schedule that had his breath caught in his throat, it was that she was making a path toward him. He stood up.

'And this would be yours.' She got to her feet with the last pile in her hand, her shining eyes looking up into his with a warmth that threatened to consume him.

It was all he could do to remain in control.

She reduced the distance, keeping her eyes fixed on his. Cass looked up into his face, her eyes soft, her lips warm and waiting.

All control left him. All thought left him. He swept Cass into his arms and claimed her mouth. All that mattered was that the woman he wanted was in his arms, her lips against his, making him feel so deeply that he felt as though he'd stop breathing.

Cassie knew it was crazy. But he felt so right. Was so right. He had to feel the same way as she did— the questions he'd asked said it all.

His lips danced with hers, his tongue plundering

and delving, exploring and tasting. She let the papers drop and they fluttered around their legs.

She wrapped her arms around him and traced the line of muscle up his back. He was as hard, as solid, and as warm as she'd imagined.

Matt groaned beneath her lips, pulling her close to his body, moulding her against him, and wrapping his arms around her.

She raked her fingers down his strong back, then worked them up, over his taut stomach, up his heaving chest, touching the soft warmth of his neck. She slipped her arms around his neck and ran her fingers through his fine hair, while his tongue made love to hers.

Cassie wanted him!

His kisses trailed down her neck, tasting her, claiming her, inciting her. His mouth persuasive, exploratory, hot, passionate.

Heat seared her body, firing her every nerve, tuning her to the thrum of his heart against his chest...

His hands traced her body, down her curves, caressing the roundness of her hips, her bottom, then up again.

His strong fingers memorised the shape of her, up her ribs, cupping the softness of her breasts.

Cassie sighed. He felt so good, so right, and she wanted so much more. She ran a hand down his back, gripping his tight butt and pulling his body hard against hers. She rubbed herself against him, the need for all of him driving her wild.

Matt pulled her up into his arms, hard against him,

striding to the bedroom. He dropped her onto the bed, yanking his shirt off in a frenzy of cloth and flying buttons.

Cassie struggled out of her windcheater and reached out for his bronzed chest. The need to touch was excruciating. She stroked his hot flesh, across his torso, tracing the shape of his muscles that rippled under her touch.

He covered her mouth with his again and she bit at his soft lips, writhing beneath him. No one had made her feel like this before. Ever.

Matt's hands plied her hips, her waist, and massaged her ribs. He slipped the vest-top up and over her head, tossing it on the floor.

He pulled back, looking at her as though she was precious. 'Oh, Cass.' He stroked her cheek with his thumb, running it along her jaw, down over the throbbing pulse at her neck, ever so slowly.

Cassie took a deep breath. Her breasts ached with the need to feel his touch and his lips, and the waiting was an exquisite torture and Matt, a master.

He traced the shape of her breast with his thumb, then cupped its fullness, stroking, worshipping. He buried his face in her hair and kissed the pounding pulse at her neck, kissed the tip of her chin, plundered the softness of her mouth, her lobes, then down the line of her neck and down.

She reached out and laced his fingers with her own, drawing him down against her. Flesh to flesh. Body to body. This was better than she'd dreamed, better than she'd imagined; this was real.

The phone pealed. One ring. Two.

'Should you get that?' Cassie whispered.

Three rings. Four.

Matt shot her a mischievous look and kissed her words away, kept kissing her. The phone fell quiet.

She explored every muscle on his chest, letting the discomfort of missing a call melt away with the glorious sensation he was evoking in her.

Matt kissed her hand, pressing his lips into her palm, tracing kisses along her fingers.

He froze. His lips pressed against her ring finger. He pulled away. 'I can't do this. Not like this.' He cupped her upturned face, searching it, and smoothed her hair, pushing the loose tendrils back.

Cassie ached. 'You did it the other night. What was so different then?' She was breathless. Her mind grappled with the overload of sensory input of his kiss, his touch, and the feel of his naked flesh.

He touched her trembling lips with one finger. 'I have to tell you, Cass. I was—'

A knock. Another one, louder.

Cassie hung on his words. She loved the sound of her name on his lips. And the depth in his eyes suggested he was going to share something meaningful, moving, and eloquent.

Matt jerked away from her. 'I've got to get that.'

'Leave it. Tell me…' Her voice came out husky and deep, her hand catching his arm. 'About the first night.'

He shook his head, brushing aside her fingers. 'It could be important.'

Cassie watched him retreat from her, turn his back on her, and move purposefully to the door as though he were escaping.

He swung the door open, shielding her from view. 'What?' His voice was harsh.

'Sorry. Sorry to disturb you, Mr Keegan, but there is an emergency—the computer has some problem. You're needed. Now.'

'I'll be right there.' Matt left the door ajar. He barely said two words to her. He put his shirt back on.

She knew he had an emergency. Logic said he'd be concerned, distracted, and tense. But she couldn't shrug off the feeling that there was more to this, more to his tense silence.

Had the guilt of the other night finally hit him or had she triggered some bad memory? She shook her head, trying to clear her thoughts. 'Want to talk about it?' She glanced toward the back of the door. The officer was probably still waiting there making conversation impossible. Was that what he'd wanted?

'I haven't got time,' he said firmly. 'You understand.'

Yes, she did. She was a businesswoman. She'd been brought up with seriously committed workaholics. But no, there was a large chunk that didn't. Her heart didn't understand. He could spare a minute, a second...

'When will you be back?' She hated the words as soon as they left her mouth. She sounded like a desperado. Wanton. And she was. Every inch of her body ached for him.

'No idea,' he threw at her, and he gripped the door handle. 'Don't wait up.'

Cassie hugged her knees to her, her mind and body numbed by the sudden change in him. Surely he had time to tell her something. Anything. Even a sweet nothing to hold her over while she waited for him to return.

She dragged in long, slow breaths. She could wait, she guessed. There was no rush. There'd be plenty of time to talk. Later. Tomorrow.

The door slammed closed. She stared at it blankly. She couldn't shake the feeling that it was her, somehow, who had caused Matt's change in mood. But for the life of her, she couldn't figure out how.

CHAPTER THIRTEEN

MATT glanced out the window, his hands resting on the keyboard on his lap. The sky was a dull grey, the stars winking out. Morning had finally arrived. He stretched his neck, trying to loosen the knots.

Cass would be lying asleep in his bed, waiting for him. He shifted restlessly on the seat. And there was nothing else he wanted more than to go to her. But he couldn't.

He wasn't hiding. He was working. Why he had to define it he wasn't sure. He wasn't afraid of what she evoked in him, it was more for her sake.

He wouldn't be good for her. Couldn't be. Not when she found out what had really happened that first night. Matt couldn't bring himself to make mad, passionate love to her, all night, without clearing the lies between them. He could have so easily. Hell, he wanted her. But he couldn't ignore the fact he'd lied to her. Hurt her. A future with Cass relied upon him coming clean. And he had to admit he had no idea at all how to do it.

He'd needed to think it through. Mull over the choice of words. Decide on the best venue, the right mood… This computer glitch was a godsend.

The screen flicked to another diagnostic. He stabbed the keyboard. Besides, work was important.

It was why he was here. He knew that. She knew that. So what was the problem? His gut rolled. He was painfully aware of his own cowardice.

He stood up abruptly and worked off his excess energy by pacing. He stared at the floor, tossing over in his mind what he would say to her, what he could say to her, so they still had a chance at being together.

Matt could almost see the scar on the carpet where he'd been walking back and forth across the room. He stopped and inhaled a deep breath.

He was human, after all. So he had guilt. That was a good thing. But, much as he mulled the idea over and over, he couldn't figure out a way to break the truth to her. And there was no way he could go back and face her until he was ready. To tell that truth, the whole truth and nothing but the truth. And the truth lay as heavily in his gut as the lie.

He clenched his jaw. She'd hate him. He knew it. And the thought sat like a brick in his chest. But he had to tell her, to try to make her understand that he'd done it for the right reasons. They couldn't have a future without coming clean.

He glanced at his watch. There was plenty of time before the ship docked. Hours. He could take her up to the Sunrise Deck and hold her in his arms, support her through the shock, kiss away the tears, give her himself to dampen Sebastian's callous treatment of her.

'Matt!' Carl's voice jarred him, the tone dire.

Matt turned. The computer screen was blank. Ice seeped into his pores. He punched a key. Nothing. He glanced at his watch. He had to get the system up and running before they came into dock. He had to.

Cassie stood out on the balcony, the wind caressing her face, staring out at the mass of land that was getting larger by the minute.

She needed a good slap in the face! She had to be delusional for considering anything with Matt Keegan, for trusting him… She was getting married in two days. Or was she?

She leant on the rail and stared at the deep blue waterway below her. She'd be damned if she was going to torment herself over him. He didn't deserve the time. If he wanted to run out the door while she was lying half naked and wanting on his bed and leave her for an entire day and another whole night…

Cassie rested her chin on her arms. Matt hadn't contacted her at all. If he cared for her as she cared for him, he'd have sent some message to her. Wouldn't he? Unless he'd fallen overboard. Her muscles tensed. Unlikely. It was more likely he was giving her a major brush-off. Or he was totally and utterly absorbed in his work. She'd been there, done that.

The breakfast tray had arrived earlier, but again no message with the attendant. She shook her head. How did Matt do it to her? After everything she'd been through she'd let herself fall for him, totally and utterly. She'd hoped to hold back a little, give herself some saving grace if he hurt her…but, goodness, when he'd been talking about love, when he'd been kissing her, touching her, loving her, what little barrier she'd had left had crumpled.

He was the one.

She loved the way his voice melted over her, and how his eyes saw right to her very soul. She loved the kind gentleness behind his words, the warmth in his eyes, and the comfort of his touch.

Cassic was through fighting it. She loved Matt Keegan. And it felt glorious. Her whole body buzzed for him, yearned for him, wanted him—totally and utterly.

If only he hadn't run off.

She pondered the coffee scroll she'd taken from his breakfast tray, willing him to come and stop her eating it. She bit into it, keeping alert for the sound of the door, for Matt… Nothing.

It was her lot in life, she guessed. She didn't get the simple guys—she got the tough ones. The ones with deep, dark secrets that interrupted their lovemaking and sent them running from the room. Her mind skipped over the possibilities and got nowhere again. She was being crazy. It was probably something simple. Probably just work.

Cassie sat down heavily in one of the chairs on their balcony and stared back at the ocean they'd crossed.

There was no doubt that there was something he was going to tell her. Something serious. Never in a million years would she have thought a man would run away from a warm, willing and able woman. But Matt had. And wondering why was bewildering.

Cassie sat bolt upright. She'd be damned if she was going to sulk over him. He didn't deserve it. Or her. If he wanted to run off on her without so much as a word…

Cassie counted down the minutes until the ship docked. There were far too many. They dragged by. She spent half of them with her eyes closed in a deck-chair on the balcony, trying not to think too much, with one ear listening for the door.

Cassie hauled herself out of the deckchair to the call of the horns announcing their arrival. Matt was out of time.

Her legs were heavy as she strode into the cabin. She dawdled into the bedroom and opened a drawer, pulling out the clothes he'd bought her.

She glanced around the cabin one last time, breathing in the salty breeze, the slight hint of Matt's cologne, and giving one last glance to the bed.

Maybe one day she'd remember the first night.

She bundled all her clothes up in the bags, trying not to ponder on why Matt was avoiding her, why he hadn't called. Could his work be so full-on that he couldn't spare a minute for a call?

It was possible that she'd become carried away with wild assumptions of his supposed feelings for her. The night before last could have been just a con-tinuation of his callous disregard for women. Her chest ached. And not something more, something special.

Cassie made her way to the foyer, keeping her attention sharp. She didn't want to miss him. Not now. Not when missing seeing him now meant the difference between a for-ever goodbye, or not. Depending...

She watched numbly as the ship moved closer to the docks. Her stomach was leaden. More than anything she wanted to tell Matt how she felt about him. And give him a chance to explain.

Cassie had seen too many movies where the heroine left not knowing what the hero really felt—wasting valuable time, or ruining the chance at love, growing old alone. *She* wasn't going to.

She loved him. The thought rocked her. She had to tell him and she'd be damned if she was going to move from this spot without telling him.

Cassie shifted restlessly, scanning the massing crowd. She'd have to inform Sebastian that the wedding was off. It would have to be cancelled. But she'd break the news face to face. It wouldn't be fair otherwise.

The docking was over in what seemed like minutes. But no Matt. He couldn't let her leave without saying anything, without a goodbye.

What would that mean? That he was working. Or he didn't care about her enough to make the effort? She swallowed hard. He knew she'd be heading home to her wedding.

He had to come and say *something*!

'Cass, going on a day trip?' Rob's voice was unmistakable, its gentle lilt hitting Cassie like a brick wall. If Rob wasn't working, was Matt working?

Cassie shook her head, unable to trust her voice. She met Rob's dark eyes, so like her brother's that Cassie's insides roiled.

Rob raised her finely arched brows. 'You're leaving?' She cocked her head to one side, her surprise unmistakable.

'Yes.' Cassie couldn't meet her eyes. 'I have plans back in Australia.' She cast a last look towards the foyer, to the people milling around, getting organised into groups for tours.

'Does it have anything to do with Matt? I know he's really moody. I don't know what it is. But he isn't normally like this.' Rob put a hand on her hip. 'He's more introspective than I've ever seen him. What's the deal with you two?'

'Nothing.' Her throat ached. It was becoming more obvious by the second it was nothing to him. He hadn't come back yesterday, or even last night. No call or message this morning. Nothing. She looked over Rob's shoulder. There was a slim chance that it was just work that was keeping him from her…but here was Rob standing in front of her.

'Really nothing?' Rob's voice rose in pitch. She tossed her hair over her shoulder. 'I haven't even seen Matt this morning. I heard he's been busy. I'm on my way up to the bridge now… I've been working on the security system half the night.'

Cassie swallowed hard. That explained how Matt could be working and she wasn't. A warmth spread through her belly. Maybe it was just work keeping him away…

Rob looked around at the crowd of people. 'I know this sounds a little forward, but haven't you been sharing a cabin with him for the last three days?'

'A cabin, yes.' Cassie's cheeks heated. 'A bed, no. Except for the first night.' Cassie couldn't help herself. She needed a shoulder to cry on. Desperately. 'Before the ship had set sail.'

Rob tucked her dark hair off her face. 'Pardon?'

Cassie moistened her lips. She took a breath. This was it. Confession time. 'Before the ship set sail, that Sunday night. I slept with Matt.'

'No, you didn't.' Rob didn't even hesitate. 'Matt didn't arrive on the ship until Monday morning. I should know, he came with us.'

'He came with you?' Cassie echoed, an icy dread seeping into her blood. Her knees threatened to give out from under her. All the stress, the worry, the guilt and she hadn't done anything with him! Tears pricked her eyes. How could he? *Why* would he? 'He came with you in the morning?' she managed, trying to keep her voice even. 'He wasn't even aboard the ship that night? Are you sure?'

'Yes. Of course I'm sure. Look, what has he been saying to you? Are you okay?' Rob put a hand on Cassie's shoulder.

Rob probably thought she was demented. Maybe she was. Why the blazes would Matt lie to her about being with her, for goodness' sake? And what the hell had happened? Why had she been in his bed? Her stomach rolled.

It didn't make sense. She shook her head. 'Look,

I've got to go.' Cassie turned away from Rob willing the ache in the back of her throat to go.

This was getting worse by the second. He didn't want to see her off, he hadn't slept with her, and he'd lied to her...the jerk had lied to her! How many lies had he fed her?

'One other thing.' Cassie turned back to the jerk's sister. 'Why wouldn't you share your cabin with me?' It would have made the trip far easier for her, would have kept her out of Matt's way, and would have saved her from embarrassing herself as she had, especially the night before last.

Rob raised her eyebrows. 'Of course you could've. All you had to do was ask.'

'Didn't Matt ask you for me?' But she already knew the answer. The chill spread to her toes.

'No. He didn't ask me at all.' Rob furrowed her brow, her eyes narrowing.

Cassie straightened and managed a stiff smile. 'I have to go now. Have a lovely time on the cruise...dancing, eating, swimming,' she said dully, forcing the words out to sound half normal.

'Swimming? I don't swim. Deadly scared of it.' She shrugged and looked away, flicking her dark hair off her shoulder.

The pieces fell into place. 'Oh, so it was you who found your brother that day in the pool,' Cassie mumbled, turning away, her mind fighting with her heart as the truth seeped into her body.

Cassie walked tall, moving through the crowd to

the walkway, her bags of clothes tucked under her arm, and headed for land.

She'd done it again. Opened herself only to get hurt again. She could never have imagined a man to stoop so low as to convince a woman she'd slept with him, then keep her in his cabin as some weird conquest. Her mind couldn't even grasp what devious plan he'd had for her. Thank goodness work had called him away.

She swiped her cheeks with the back of her hand. She stared at the moist skin. She was crying!

It was the first time she'd cried in five years!

She smothered a sob. This was so unfair. She loved him. Really, truly loved him.

Why did she let herself feel? It only led to one thing, and she was feeling it now, keenly. Her heart was cracking in two.

She sucked in a long, slow breath. He didn't deserve tears. He really didn't. As Tom didn't. As her parents' marriage didn't. It wasn't her fault. Just theirs. Their fault for making mistakes. Not caring about her enough.

Cassie hesitated at the top of the walkway. Matt wasn't anywhere to be seen. A big part of her desperately wanted to give him a chance to explain to her, to give him a chance to make it right. There had to be some perfectly reasonable explanation for this. Had to be.

A porter rushed up. 'Miss Win? Mr Keegan asked me to give you these—and wish you a safe journey home.'

Cassie stared down at the papers pressed into her hand. The details were neatly laid out for her. The name of a charter flight to get her to Christchurch Airport, the details for a plane ticket back to Australia waiting at the terminal for her. All paid for. And a wish for a safe trip home. Out of his life.

That was it, then. He couldn't have made it any clearer. He'd lied, used her and dumped her.

She lifted her chin. She *was* going. Back to her normal safe life. Back to Sebastian. Nothing had happened that first night. Nothing eventuated from that last night.

She saw a courier in uniform standing at the dock, a small flat envelope in hand. She walked stiffly down to him, wishing she'd had the foresight to ask Eva to send her planner as well as her passport. She could have spent the long trip home rescheduling and arranging her life again.

Cassie took the envelope from the courier. Her wedding was only two days away. And now nothing stood in the way.

CHAPTER FOURTEEN

MATT shifted in his seat and glanced towards the door. He glanced at his watch. Where the hell had all the time gone? They'd been docked for ages.

He bit his lip and stabbed another button. There was no way he could leave until the system was in full operation. They'd managed to get enough systems running to dock the liner but he couldn't leave it until it was right. He darted a look to the officers on the bridge. No way he could sneak away, not if his company was going to have a future.

Cass had to know he was still working, know that he'd been trying to get away for ages. Sure, he'd used it as an excuse to escape for a while, but he'd figured out now how to confess. How to tell her what he'd instigated against her. And she had to understand. Especially since she knew Rob. She'd understand when he told her how he'd had no other choice but to lie to her to save his sister from her past. She had to.

His guts ached. He wanted to find her now. Go to her. Make it all okay. He looked towards the doorway. He had to.

He rubbed his hands over his eyes. Was this what his parents were always going on about? They'd married after a love-at-first-sight encounter. *Was* this love?

Someone shoved another cup of coffee towards him. 'I gave your lady her ticket details, sir. As requested.'

Matt jerked his head up. 'What?'

The young officer stiffened. 'I did as you instructed. I got all the details of her flights and booked them to your card and gave them to her.'

Matt swallowed. 'She's gone?'

'Yes, sir.' The man pasted a smile on his face. 'I saw her off myself.'

She had left. Without a word. Matt rolled his shoulders, a deep pain stirring in his chest.

What the hell should he do? Cass had obviously not wanted to interrupt his work, didn't want to put herself on the line again. But she was going back to Sebastian without a clue as to what really went on here.

The man coughed. 'Don't worry, Mr Keegan. I wished her a pleasant trip on your behalf.'

Matt grimaced and ran a hand through his hair. 'Thanks.' His gut tensed. She would have thought he was getting rid of her. Damn it.

He stood at the window and gazed out until his coffee grew cold in the cup. The computers were all sorted out. Back in form. Carl and Trent were monitoring for any more anomalies.

'*I* found him in the pool?' His sister's voice was unmistakable.

Matt turned, his blood chilling at the sight of his

sister's ashen face, her shining eyes filled with tears. 'Pardon?'

'Don't act innocent,' Rob choked. 'I've put it all together. I was the one who found him. That's why I can't remember…why I can't stand swimming… because I couldn't save him. If only I'd known how to resuscitate him…'

Matt stepped forward and wrapped his sister's trembling body in his arms. 'It was an accident, there was nothing we could do,' he whispered, his voice thick and unsteady. How did she find out?

She sagged at the knees and he lowered her to the floor where he held her while the sobs racked her body.

Carl and Trent shot Matt some hand signals that they were heading out for some food. Matt nodded.

'Why didn't anyone tell me?' she croaked.

'You were young. You didn't remember. We thought it best that way.'

'We?'

'Mum and Dad. They decided that it was best for you not to remember the details, so they kept it from you. The more time passed, the easier it got to believing it didn't really happen at all.' Matt faltered. Rob was handling it…Rob was handling some of the truth. But could she handle the rest? He sucked in a deep breath, fighting the nausea in the pit of his gut. She would never have to, if he had anything to do with it.

Rob swiped her cheeks and pulled out of his arms. 'I think I'll go and freshen up, and do some thinking.'

'You okay?' Matt let her go, reluctantly. The urge to protect her from the truth, the whole truth, was as strong now as it had ever been, if not more.

'No, but I think I will be.' Rob stood up and smoothed the creases out of her clothes.

Matt got to his feet and stared out the window at the town, steeling himself against the emotions threatening to swamp him. He felt just as strongly about protecting Cass from Sebastian... Why in hell had he let her go?

Rob sniffled. 'Pining already?'

He didn't turn, the weight in his chest was almost too much to even breathe at the thought of Cassie and what he'd let slip through his fingers. 'You saw her go?'

She came up beside him, still wiping moisture from her eyes. 'Yes. And she didn't look too happy. What did you do?'

He leant heavily on the wall. 'What didn't I do?'

She wrapped a hand over his. 'Okay. So you mucked it up. The real question is, what are you going to do now?'

He straightened. Rob was right. It wasn't over. He looked longingly at the town, the airport was there, somewhere.

It would be so easy just to walk off the ship, but he had a job to do. So what if he raced after her and told her the truth? She wouldn't give him the time of day after he told her how he'd lied about being with her that first night.

Never had he regretted a lie more than that one.

Would Cass even stop to listen to why he'd had to do it? His gut rolled and he clenched his fists against the guilt twisting around his heart.

He couldn't have Sebastian blurting out the truth to Rob about that day. Cass would have to see that. It could destroy his little sister...

Matt turned back to the computers. There was plenty of time. Cass would confess to Sebastian about the first night and there'd be no wedding. Maybe in a few months, when things quietened down, when she wasn't feeling quite so strongly about things, he could accidentally bump into her somewhere.

He smiled. The tension in his body eased. That was his plan, then. To let her cool off and somehow slip back into her life. He threw back his shoulders and strode back to the computers.

Matt punched a key on his terminal. Keeping busy was the answer to all his problems. With his mind fully engaged he wouldn't have a chance to dwell on the events of the last couple of days, on how sweet she tasted, or on how hurt Cass would be if she knew the truth. Work was the answer. He wouldn't have to think about her at all.

Trying to forget Cass was like trying to hold your breath. In short stints only. For a minute or two. Visions of her were haunting him every time he closed his eyes, every time he stopped to think, every time someone approached him.

Setting sail and leaving Dunedin behind had little effect on reducing Cass's monopoly of his thoughts.

Matt paced the floor behind his team. Ironically the computers had behaved perfectly since Dunedin. He would've preferred a challenge. Something to keep his mind occupied, busy, off the memories.

He imagined her getting on the small plane, coming here, to Christchurch, flying off into the clouds, away from the ship, away from him, to a welcome that would be nothing like she expected.

He clenched his jaw. He should have told her. Warned her what she was walking back into. What had possessed him to keep the truth from her? He'd all but guaranteed her hating him for ever.

Matt strode away from the terminals, gazing out at the brilliant blue sky. The bugs were all ironed out in the new system. The worst was over for the crew, but not for him.

His feet led him to the Sunrise Deck. He leant heavily on the rail and stared at the town of Lyttelton, knowing Christchurch and its international airport weren't far away. It was so tempting to get off and go after her. But he wouldn't. She'd be home by now.

He wasn't going to add to her troubles. After all, she really loved that damned Sebastian. That description of how she felt about him in their cabin that last night…it made his guts ache to think about it.

Then there was them. Touching, kissing. His chest hurt. He couldn't fathom what had gone through her mind. Had he pressured her? Had the lie motivated her? He shook his head. Nothing made sense.

An officer approached him. 'Phone call for you, Mr Keegan.'

His heart skipped. Maybe it was *Cass*.

Matt followed the officer to the phone, almost walking on the man's heels in his haste, his mind tossing around what she might say, what he could say in return.

'Matt Keegan.' He held his breath.

'Keegan.' A man's voice, cultured, nasal. 'It's Sebastian Browning-Smith. We seem to have a slight problem.'

Matt expelled his breath. 'And what would that be?' he responded sharply, abandoning all pretence of civility. This was the creep himself. What had he done to Cass now?

'That Cassandra hasn't confessed anything at all to me.' His voice was cold and lashing. 'You know our little arrangement. Well, it seems that your end of the deal hasn't been fulfilled and I may find it necessary to make a phone call to a certain party. Unless you help out.'

Matt fisted his hands. 'I don't see what I can do.' He was damned if he'd hurt Cass any more than he already had.

'The wedding is tomorrow. You come and attend. Yes...yes.' His voice pitched in enthusiasm. 'You come and when the minister says that hold their peace stuff you pipe up and tell the world.'

'Tell the world what exactly?' The words seared his throat, his blood raging, and his grip on the phone turning his knuckles white.

'That you slept with my fiancée.'

Sebastian could have been ordering dinner—he was

so damned casual about hurting Cass. Matt clenched his teeth, fighting the storm of curses that he wanted to spit at the man who could so callously treat another human being this way. Sebastian had no idea what he was asking of him. 'I…don't…think…so.'

'Oh, I do. I think it's perfect.' His mood was buoyant. 'Right there in front of the media.'

'And her family,' Matt bit out. Didn't the guy have any conscience?

Sebastian didn't seem to hear. 'I've arranged the flight. I'll have someone meet you at the airport and take you to a hotel. The wedding's at one.'

'But—' Fury choked him. The clunk of the receiver reverberated in Matt's ear.

Now what was he meant to do? Matt stiffened. If she was going to hate him before, she was going to hate him even more if he stood up in church in front of her family, friends and the press and plastered her reputation to the proverbial wall. But what else could he do?

CHAPTER FIFTEEN

EVA leant close to Cassie and stared out the side window of the church with her. 'What are you looking for?'

Cassie turned away. 'Something that's not coming.'

She straightened her white dress, fluffing out the skirts to keep her hands busy. She tried to smile but her heart wasn't in it. Her eyes kept darting to the door. She couldn't stop them. Something deep inside her prayed. For what exactly, she wasn't sure.

It wasn't as if a knight in shining armour were going to burst through the door and take her away, make everything all right. Her knight was a jerk. A big, fat, opportunistic jerk that had twisted her mind, and body, into knots.

Cassie had dissected the whole incident. She'd had plenty of time to think about Matt in the last two days, since the plane trip home. How Matt must have cooked up some elaborate scheme when he'd found her in his cabin that first morning. Probably to convince her to sleep with him with minimal effort on his part. It was the only answer she could come up with. To the only question that tortured her: *why?*

She swallowed the dry ache in the back of her throat. She had to pull herself together. She was getting married. In an hour's time she'd be Mrs Browning-Smith.

Eva laid a cool hand on her arm. 'I'm here for you if you want to talk about anything.' She gave Cassie a brittle smile.

'Thanks, Eva.' Cassie moved a little further away from the woman. 'But, no. There's nothing to say.' *To you.* Where were her other friends? She needed a shoulder again to cry on… 'Where's Linda?'

'Linda?' Eva's eyes narrowed. 'I've got her organising the best men into position.'

'Where's Christine?' She'd understand. She'd talked to her earlier. Told her what had happened. Her friend had listened to the whole sordid story and given her what comfort she could, but her arms were nothing like Matt's. And for some insane reason, that was all she wanted. Matt's arms around her.

Christine had advised that she postpone the wedding until Cassie had had time to think. But think about what? The facts were the facts. Matt Keegan was a lying opportunist and she was getting married to a wonderful, successful man who was perfect for her.

It didn't matter that Matt's eyes had been deep, dark and sensuous. Or that his hands had been strong and gentle. Or that she yearned to be taken into the warmth of his arms and just held, for ever.

'Christine is in charge of the flower girls. She's allocating flowers and sorting out the pecking order.'

'You have been busy organising everything.' Cassie sighed. And everybody, so that there was no one to talk to except her. But despite all the niceties Eva tossed her way, Cassie had never hit it off with Eva.

Eva smoothed out Cassie's veil and pinned it to her hair. 'Did something happen on the ship that you need to talk through?'

The question stabbed her deep in her chest. Was she that transparent? Her spirits sank lower. She'd tried so hard to behave normally, go through the usual routines, but it had to show. She hadn't even been able to bring herself to see Sebastian before the wedding... But Sebastian must have heard the change in her voice in their phone conversations because he was grilling her with all sorts of weird questions about her unexpected vacation.

Cassie was doing her best at denying it had all happened, to herself and everybody else. If she didn't stop to feel the void inside her she could have believed the last few days weren't real, that nothing had happened. That it had been a dream, or a nasty nightmare that she could do without remembering.

She almost laughed. There she'd been trying to remember a night that had never happened. What an idiot she must have looked. What a laugh Matt must have had over her trying to recall an interlude with him that had never been. She dug her nails into her palms.

Eva stepped back and perused the finished effect. She looked her in the face. 'Are you happy?'

'Ecstatic,' Cassie lied. And she would be, she was sure, in time. Once Matt had worn off, she and

Sebastian would be ecstatically happy in their suburban home with their two children and white brick wall out front.

Cassie gripped the bouquet tightly to still her trembling hands and turned back to the window. There was no point in spoiling the wedding for anyone else. She was right in the first place. Marry for logic. The right man with the right job, with the right family and interests, and she'd be right.

From her vantage point she could see everyone arriving. Her parents arrived separately, of course. They'd almost run into each other alighting from their taxis. Cassie had seen the stiffness, the forced facial expressions as they'd spoken to each other, as though they'd stepped into a boxing ring. How could they do that to each other when once, a long time ago, they'd loved each other?

All those years they'd been together, living a lie for everyone around them while they'd suppressed their true feelings. Cassie straightened tall and pulled back her shoulders, lifting her chin. She didn't want that for herself. There was no way she was going to let love turn to something like that.

The door flung open.

Cassie swung around, dropping the bouquet. Her mother strode in, looking marvellous in a deep blue suit. She sighed. 'Mum.'

'You can't imagine the flight over...I feel so jet-lagged. And the traffic getting here—' Her mother darted forward and started fussing with her hair. 'Just look at you. My little girl all grown up and getting married.'

'I'll leave you two to it.' Eva backed off. 'I'll make sure the girls are ready.'

'Mum,' she whispered, her voice hoarse. She could so easily cry. She hadn't seen her mother in months. Her mother should know what to do, should understand, should help. Tears burned in her eyes. She had to tell her, had to explain…but no sense came, just a jumble of words, tangled with choking emotions.

'What's all this in aid of? Oh, darling. What's the matter?'

Cassie shook her head. How could she possibly tell her mother what had gone on in the last week? What would she think of her? That she was stupid for believing Matt's lies, for wanting him, for opening her heart to a guy out to break it.

'Is it the wedding, dear? Nerves?'

It was far more than nerves. She wanted someone to tell her she was doing the right thing. That marrying Sebastian because he was the 'right' man was the best thing for her. That it would all work out!

She didn't want to end up alone because she'd waited for someone she really, truly loved, someone who had the power to hurt as her parents had hurt each other.

She opened her mouth.

The door swung open again.

Cassie spun around.

'It's time,' Eva announced.

A sick yearning twisted and turned inside her. She turned to her mother. 'Mum?'

'Go on.' Her mother dabbed her face lightly with

her handkerchief and pushed her towards the door, thrusting the bouquet in her hands. 'He's out there waiting for you.'

Cassie forced her legs to move. This was it. This was what she'd always wanted. The ideal man was going to be her husband—the happiest day of her life.

She closed her eyes, her heart aching.

She was doing the right thing. With the right man. For the right reasons. She would marry Sebastian Browning-Smith and to hell with Matt Keegan. He was just another opportunist.

She gave a resigned shrug and stepped through the door to the foyer. Her life was hers, under control and going as planned.

She'd never see Matt Keegan again.

There was a row of seven glorious stained-glass windows showing images of Christ. The colours were bold, standing out from the pale walls, driving home the sanctity of the place.

Seven candles adorned a large candelabra on either side of the altar, the timber pulpit between. Matt sat on a hard wooden pew, waiting amongst the strangers for the woman who'd stolen his heart.

He couldn't miss Sebastian waiting nervously at the front of the church. His four best men all wore tuxedos, too. He could tell they were related…the receding hair had to be a family trait. The range of height looked to have been orchestrated, graduating from the shortest to the tallest.

The white roses on their lapels gave them an extra flair that wasn't lost on Matt. It was picture perfect. Staged.

Matt shifted in his seat. Cass couldn't be happy with Sebastian. Could she? The painful knowledge that it was what she wanted sat heavily in his chest. Matt had already done enough to the poor woman. It was obvious that, despite what had happened with him, she desperately wanted to marry Sebastian.

Cass didn't deserve any further intrusions from Matt. She deserved to be happy. And if she wanted Sebastian that much…who was he to deny her that?

He'd thought about staying on the ship, about missing the flight, missing the wedding, but he was drawn. He had to see this through. For his sake.

He shook his head. At least he'd taken Rob out of the picture. The job on the ship was all but over and he'd insisted she take a very early, long service leave. The Greek islands would be lovely this time of year. It would give her time alone, to grieve for her little brother in peace. Well away from Sebastian and what he might throw her way. It gave him the opportunity to do right by Cass. But what the hell was right?

Matt was confused. It should have been simple having Rob's past out of the picture. He could just leave Sebastian and Cass to sort their relationship out themselves.

His heart pounded in his chest, his eyes darting to the entrance. It was only a matter of minutes now.

Eva, the woman who'd set Cassie up that first night, strode towards him. 'You look like a fish out of water,' she whispered harshly at him. 'Smile. It's a wedding.' She handed him a video camera. 'At least try to blend in. You can film it for a while, and it helps hide you. If she sees you beforehand it could ruin everything.' She strode down to the front of the church, issuing orders to other people.

Matt stared at the camera. He had to film it? He ran the lens over the church, over the ornate lattice-work of the balcony above him, the vines twisted and turned in an intricate pattern, painted cream with a gloriously polished timber rail above. He felt just as twisted.

The church was all carved timber, teak probably. With faded patterned carpet that had seen better days. He filmed it all. Why not? It kept him busy.

The start of the organ music jerked him from his thoughts. The music stopped. Teasing him. Taunting him. A murmur of voices rose all around him—whispers he couldn't hear. Had Cass changed her mind? A warmth filled him.

He crossed his fingers. It would save her from so much if she called it off now, before she entered the church. Matt turned, watching the doors at the top of the stairs for any sign of the bride.

The music started in earnest. There was no mistaking the bridal march this time.

A cold knot formed in Matt's stomach, his breathing shallow, quick, unsteady.

Four bridesmaids came first with long pink dresses, tightly fitted to their bodies. Each had a bunch of co-ordinating flowers in their hands. They moved slowly, stepping down the stairs in time with the march. He filmed them all. It seemed easier to believe he was here to enjoy the wedding, to film it as some impartial observer would, rather than dwelling on, or dealing with, why he was really here.

Cass stepped into the church. Her white gown fell

around her like a bell, the pure white fabric swishing about her as she moved towards the altar. Like a lamb to the slaughter.

She seemed tentative. Matt guessed she was nervous. He zoomed in. She looked absolutely gorgeous, like an angel in white, but her eyes were cast down, her chin low, mindless, it seemed, of the cameras flashing around her.

She stepped up to the pulpit. A man, her father, handed her to Sebastian. Matt hadn't even noticed the greying gentleman beside her. Or anything else.

'Who presents this woman to be married?' The minister wasn't wasting time.

'I do.' Cass's father cast her an encouraging smile.

'We have come together in the sight of God for the joining in marriage of this man, Sebastian, and this woman, Cassandra.'

Matt swallowed hard, the blood rushing to his head. He couldn't do this. He couldn't let her marry him, no matter how much she wanted to. He knew it wouldn't last. He knew the slimy creep didn't love her at all, knew he would marry her anyway and wait until after the elections to make his next move.

His chest ached. But if she wanted to marry him, Matt had to let it be. He wanted the best for her. Wanted her to be happy.

'What therefore God has joined together, let no one put asunder.'

But *he* loved her.

'So that children may be born and nurtured in secure and loving care for their well-being and instruction and for the good order of society, to the glory of God.'

His children, *not* Sebastian's. The thought riled him. He couldn't let her make a mistake like this. He clenched his fists by his side.

'Cassandra and Sebastian have now come here to be joined in holy union in which God has led them.'

But if he interrupted the wedding she'd never forgive him. But if he didn't, she'd marry Sebastian. Either way he lost her.

'They seek his blessing on their life together…'

But could he stop the wedding? Was it in him to do it? He lowered the video camera and stared at the marriage party. It was more real, more tangible, more terrifying.

'If any person here can show why they may not lawfully be joined in marriage they should speak now—'

Matt jumped to his feet.

Several heads turned towards him.

'Or hereafter remain in silence.'

This was it. The biggest choice of his life. To say nothing and let her marry Sebastian Browning-Smith, or tell the truth and lose her.

Matt took a deep breath.

CHAPTER SIXTEEN

'I CAN.' Matt's voice came out weak, shaky. 'Me,' he said with more force. 'I say no.'

'Pardon?' The minister looked directly at Matt, then around him wildly for guidance. The whole party turned toward Matt.

No one moved. No one spoke. The minister glared at Matt, looking perplexed about what to do next.

Matt met Cassie's wide eyes. He tried to read them, see what she was feeling, but he couldn't tell. Not at all. His gut tossed. Was he doing the right thing?

The minister furrowed his brow. 'This is a serious accusation, young man—are you sure?'

He didn't drop his eyes from Cassie's. 'I am.'

'Then what say you?' the minister demanded.

'I say—' Matt took another breath. '—that Cassandra cannot marry Sebastian Browning-Smith because…' his chest ached with the power of his feelings '…because *I* love her.'

Cassie's breath caught in her throat. Her chest felt as if it were going to explode. *He loved her.* Tears sprang to her eyes. His love was what she wanted. What she yearned for. What she'd prayed for. But could she trust him? Or was all this just a continuation of his game?

The minister turned to her. 'We can have him removed and taken out,' he whispered.

Sebastian turned to her, puffing out his chest indignantly. 'No, I want to hear what he has to say.' He glared at her. 'How can he love you, Cassandra? What's been going on?'

She shuddered at his accusation. She should have told him what had happened. Sebastian didn't deserve this embarrassment, not here, not like this, because she couldn't bring herself to confess her own stupidity to him.

'I think it would be best,' the priest said loudly, 'to take a short recess and get this business sorted.' He pulled at the collar of his robe.

Cassie strode into the back room, following Sebastian's rigid back. She was a selfish fool. The poor man. How could she do this to him? How could Matt do this to him? To her.

The events on the ship flooded back to her again. Their conversations, their interactions, the exposing of his lies!

Her blood heated. What was she thinking? He couldn't love her. *He'd lied to her.*

She turned and faced him, the room feeling far too small for her. It looked like an office-cum-storeroom, cluttered with chairs and statues, but with a minister, a grouchy groom, an interloper and her, almost a bride.

Cassie couldn't miss the way Matt's black suit was perfectly tailored around his wide shoulders, slim hips and long legs. He didn't wear a tie with the white shirt he wore underneath. His top button was undone reminding her of the chest she'd touched, caressed and kissed. His rusty brown hair was combed back, his dark eyes holding hers.

Cassie's body ached. 'Talk quick, Keegan,' she bit out, fighting the despair tearing at her heart. 'The meter is running.'

He faltered, moving a camera from one hand to the other. 'I had to tell you—' He looked at his shoes, then up again, piercing her with his intensity. 'I love you.'

A warmth caressed her heart, for a moment. 'What do you know of love?' she challenged, clutching the bouquet close to her chest.

'What's been going on with you two?' Sebastian moved backwards, looking towards the minister, who stood with his hands clenched tightly in front of him, his eyes on the door. 'How do you even know this man, Cassandra?' Sebastian's brow furrowed. 'Did something happen on that ship?'

'No.' Cassie squeezed the bouquet tighter. 'Nothing happened. Did it?' She shot Matt an accusing glare.

'Look, maybe we should have a minute alone,' Matt suggested, giving Sebastian a long, hard look. He put the camera down onto one of the stacks of chairs.

'I think that might be best.' Sebastian took the minister's arm and led him to the door. 'You're okay with that, aren't you, honey?'

Cassie didn't argue. She had quite a few things to

say to Matt Keegan and none of them she could say in front of Sebastian without hurting him. She was glad he was being so understanding, reminding her again why she was going to marry him.

Sebastian opened the door, his hand on the minister's back propelling him out of the room.

The minister frowned at both Cassie and Matt. 'This is most irregular.'

The door closed.

Cassie watched Matt warily. There was no way she was going to blindly accept a word that came out of his mouth. *Fool me once, shame on you. Fool me twice, shame on me.*

'I have to tell you—I lied to you that first day.' Matt strode toward her, reducing the distance between them. 'I didn't sleep with you.'

'You didn't?' She raised her eyebrows in mock surprise and stepped back. She damn well *knew* he hadn't. And if she could think over the pounding of her heart, the wild frenzy in her mind, now was her chance to find out why. 'I don't understand,' she said innocently. 'Then why?'

He stopped an arm's length from her. 'It's complicated.' He ran a hand through his hair, staring at his shoes.

'I'm all ears.' She lifted her arm in an exaggerated fashion and cast a pointed look at her watch on her wrist. She wasn't going to give the liar an inch.

'I was blackmailed.'

She managed a laugh and turned on her heel. 'If that's the best you can do…?'

Matt grabbed her arm. 'It's true. Rob didn't know she was involved in our brother dying. She couldn't remember so we were keeping it from her. Until you put the pieces together and blurted it out.'

'Oh?' Cassie brushed his hand away, stifling the chaos his touch caused in her body, and stalked to the door. She took the handle, finding comfort in the cold steel of it beneath her shaking fingers, knowing her big mouth must have devastated Rob.

He followed her. 'The truth could destroy her.'

'Did it?' Cassie whispered, her stomach tossing at her own stupidity.

'No.' Matt shook his head, moving closer still. 'But you have to understand… Rob wasn't just the one who found Brendan—she was the one *looking after him*. She was babysitting our little brother and got distracted and he drowned. She's blocked out the memory. So, can't you see why protecting her from the truth is important to me?'

Cassie averted her eyes, her heart aching for Matt, for the little boy who had lost his life, and for Rob who didn't deserve that burden. 'But aren't I important too?' she whispered. 'Aren't I worth the truth?'

'Hell, yes.' Matt cupped her face with his warm hands. 'You're the most beautiful woman I've ever met. You deserve the world. That's why I'm here.'

Cassie pulled out of his grasp and stared at his hands, trying to ignore the throb of her heart, trying to ignore how close his face was to hers, how his eyes were so bright and vulnerable. 'I don't see the world. Or the truth.'

He'd lied to her. He'd put her through all that agony and pain for nothing. She pursed her lips. If only he'd just told her… 'I don't see anything like the truth!'

'I need you to understand.' Matt dropped his hands to his sides. He looked to the ceiling, clearing his throat. 'I couldn't let Rob suffer.'

Cassie pressed her back hard against the door. She knew that. She didn't want Rob to suffer either. What did he think she was? Heartless? 'And someone knew all this and blackmailed you?' She turned the handle on the door, her mind a wild frenzy of confusion and doubt. She shook her head, trying to clear her thoughts. 'I can't see that any of it has anything to do with me.'

Matt put a hand up, pushing it against the door, leaning over her, holding it closed. 'I brought a friend home from school that day. We came on the late bus and mucked around on the way home.'

Cassie could see the pain etched in his face.

'We were too late. Way too late. But my friend—' he paused '—was Sebastian.'

She managed a smile. 'No.' She shook her head.

'He didn't want to break off his engagement to you because of his ratings—he relied on your honesty. It was a set-up. I was to say I'd slept with you. You'd go racing to him and confess. Then he'd get all the voters' sympathies.'

'Sebastian?' Cassie sidestepped Matt, backing away from the door, from him, his words seeping slowly into her mind. How could he make up such a story? 'No!'

'It's the truth. Why would I lie?'

Could it be true? Cassie chewed her lip. Would Sebastian have set her up? An icy chill seeped into her body. 'I didn't tell Sebastian...'

'So he told me to come to the church and announce it in front of everyone.' Matt watched her, his face stricken.

'And you did.' She took a gulp of air. Matt had set her up, twice. Cassie straightened. 'Congratulations, Matt. You did your job well. I hope you have a great life.' She took a deep breath. 'Now get out!'

CHAPTER SEVENTEEN

'CASS?' Matt grabbed her arm and turned her to face him.

Cassie looked up at him, her eyes annoyingly close to tears. 'You've done your job. Your performance was flawless.' She wrenched her arm from his grip. 'Go back to your own life and get out of mine.'

'I'm not leaving. Not until you understand. It wasn't like that...'

Cassie leant against the wall, her mind a jumble of thoughts. She understood already. It was all a lie. Everything! She didn't want to believe it. Couldn't. Not sweet Sebastian. 'It can't be true. Sebastian wasn't even there at my hen-night.'

Matt held his hands stiffly at his sides. 'He had help.'

Realisation hit her full force in the chest. 'Eva gave me that cocktail.' Pain choked her. She pushed a strand of hair back from her eyes, her fingers colliding with the hair comb that held her veil in place. Cassie wrenched it off her head and tossed it aside. 'She drugged me, didn't she?'

'I didn't know. Honestly.' Matt's voice was soft and gentle. 'The plan didn't include you sleeping through the ship setting sail. That was my fault. I'm sorry. I couldn't bring myself to wake you.'

Cassie stood still. She couldn't quite take it in. It sounded so unreal, but Matt sounded genuine. The truth was still the truth, though. Matt Keegan had lied to her.

The door swung open. 'Okay, I've been patient enough. What the blazes is going on?' Sebastian strode into the room. 'Who the hell is this guy?'

Cassie turned. She moved her mouth but she just couldn't form the words. Eva appeared behind Sebastian. The longing gaze she gave Sebastian confirmed Matt's theory. It all fell into place. She clenched her fists. 'I won't be marrying you, Sebastian.'

Sebastian's eyes widened in mock surprise. 'Why, darling?' he managed in a *faux*-innocent, greasy tone. 'I love you. We have all the guests waiting. The press…'

She took a breath, ready to let rip on him, but she caught Matt's dark eyes and held her tirade. She couldn't let Rob suffer, or anyone else for that matter, over this. 'I don't love you any more, Sebastian.'

'Oh, goodness me,' Eva sighed. 'What a disaster. With all your family and the press…'

Sebastian cast a glance at Eva. She would have done a drama academy proud.

Cassie stared down at the folds of her beautiful white wedding gown—the one she'd dreamt of wearing on her perfect day for ever so long—and stroked the smooth, cool satin. It was so obvious now. She'd been naïve and innocent, accepting everything Sebastian had said to her, everything that Eva had arranged. And Sebastian's connection to the cruise ship that had enabled her to have her party there in the first place was standing right in front of her. Matt.

They'd used her. Played her like a doll. And now, she was left with nothing. She glanced at Matt. Absolutely nothing. The only reason Matt was bound to her was because of his sister.

'Please, darling, surely there must be something I can do. Something I can say to make you change your mind.' Sebastian was putting on a great performance.

Cassie's skin crawled at how easily he could lie to her. She'd nearly made the worst mistake of her life!

She watched Sebastian leave the small alcove, his shoulders slumped over, his head down. She didn't miss the sound of the crowd in the church, their voices, murmuring. She could guess what they were saying, what they were thinking.

She turned to Matt. 'Thank you for telling me the truth,' she said with an air of calm she wished ran deeper. 'I appreciate your honesty, however belated.' Her mind touched on how different everything would have been if he'd confessed on the ship, before she'd come racing back to make a fool of herself.

Matt moved closer to her. 'I didn't just do it for Rob.'

'Oh, really?' she scoffed. 'Warrant me with some intelligence.' Cassie fluffed up her skirts. 'Next you'll be telling me you did it for me.'

'No. I did it for myself.' He put a hand on each of her shoulders. 'I *do* love you.'

Her stomach coiled tight. 'You can stop the act.

Your part is played.' She darted a look into his soft eyes, willing her heart to stay cold. 'You can go home and pick up your life where you left off.'

He shook his head. 'Not without you.'

She stiffened. 'You've lied to me, tried to conceal the truth from me, seduced me and now…now this.' She swung her arms wide. 'I'm not going anywhere with you.'

Matt pulled her against his solid body and kissed her, smothering her protests.

His lips were as warm and persuasive as she remembered and her blood fired to the call of his body, the promise in his kiss.

Matt pulled away. 'Now?'

Her senses reeled. How could he do so much damage to her control in so few seconds? All the barriers she'd put in place were demolished, leaving her vulnerable, insecure.

She pursed her lips, steeling herself against the ache in her body, the pain in her chest. 'Have you quite finished?' There was no way she was going to fall for his charm again, only to be hurt. 'If that's all?'

Matt took a step backward. 'I'm not leaving unless you tell me that you don't love me.' He crossed his arms. 'I want to hear from your own lips that you don't feel anything for me.'

She didn't hesitate. She couldn't afford to. Looking at the floor, she whispered, 'I don't love you.' And she turned her back on him, plucking the petals off the flowers in her bouquet.

Cassie heard his heavy footfalls, heard his momentary pause at the door. Heard the door open, slam shut. That was it. Her brief and torturous fling with Matt Keegan was well and truly over.

She let the tears fall unchecked, the all-consuming ache in her chest making her knees buckle beneath her. She sagged into a white, fluffy heap on the floor. If only she knew if she'd made the right decision.

Cassie stumbled into the room where she'd changed into her gown such a short time before, aeons ago in her mind.

Men were all alike. Her fingers fumbled with the fasteners of her wedding gown. They couldn't be trusted. Not a single one.

'Honey, what on earth is going on?' Her mother's voice was high as she rushed in, slamming the door closed behind her.

She swiped her wet cheeks. This was just what she didn't need. Her mother to point out how she should have realised she was being duped, where she'd acted like a stupid idiot, all the reasons why her highly intelligent mother wouldn't have fallen into the same situation. 'Not now, Mum.'

'But you loved Sebastian, didn't you?' Her mum turned her around and undid the dress. It fell to the floor.

Cassie swung around and kicked the dress away from her. 'No, Mother, I didn't. I decided to marry someone that was right for me, figuring logic would give me a better chance at making the distance than all that lovey-dovey mush, but look where I am.' She gave a short laugh. 'I didn't even make it to *I do*.'

'Why?' She bent and picked up the white gown. 'Why wouldn't you choose someone that you loved?'

Cassie was tired. Sick of being tactful. All out of polite excuses. 'Because I didn't want to end up like you and Dad.'

'Oh, darling.' Her mother pulled her into her arms.

Cassie couldn't keep her pain in any longer. Hot tears slid down her cheeks…she knew the comfort of her mother's arms couldn't keep reality at bay. She had to face her own life. She wasn't a child any more.

She managed a half-choked laugh. 'I'm sorry. I'm such a mess, Mum. I didn't want to remind you.'

'Darling.' She hugged her tighter. 'Your father and I got married because we thought being good friends was enough.' Her mother rubbed her back. 'We suited each other. I grew to love him, honey, but it made sense…we were both going to be teachers, liked the same things, had the same views.'

Cassie pulled back. 'Just like Sebastian and I?' Her mind reeled at the irony. All these years she'd been trying to avoid her parents' path of a doomed marriage when her premise had been all wrong. 'Oh, Mum. What have I done? I just told the man I love to get lost.'

'If you really love him, it won't matter.' Her mother nodded, her eyes bright. 'Go after him, honey.'

Cassie moved to the door, grabbing the handle. She was an idiot. Everything that she'd planned so carefully with Sebastian to make her life perfect would have left her with the same situation as her parents!

'Darling.' Her mother's voice was soft but firm.

Cassie turned.

'You might like to get dressed first.'

Cassie looked down and managed a smile. The media would have loved that. Not only did they have the juicy gossip of Sebastian's wedding turning into a disaster, but to have her running around in her lacy underwear…

She pulled on the clothes she'd come in. A pair of jeans and a shirt. She shook her hair out of the plastered perfection the hairdresser had created and took off the pearl drops at her ears. She was ready to meet her destiny.

Her mum hung her wedding dress back onto its hanger. 'Where's your veil, honey?'

'Does it matter?' She slipped her handbag over her shoulder. She wasn't going to get caught without her purse again, ever. She'd found it tucked into one of the presents a friend had given her. She could almost remember doing it, the image hazy, fogged by the drugs, when she'd been packing up the presents with Eva. If only Eva had known… How things would have been different if she'd had it with her, if Matt had woken her up, if she'd gone home before the ship had set sail…

'You might want your veil.' Her mother offered her a soft smile. 'For next time.'

Cassie's heart skipped. Maybe, it wouldn't be too far away. Maybe. 'In that little side room.' She wrenched open the door and froze. 'I don't know where to find him.'

'Someone has to know.'

And Cassie knew exactly who. The man she never wanted to see again, the man behind the whole scheme, Sebastian Browning-Smith.

CHAPTER EIGHTEEN

MATT should have known. How he'd imagined they could have some kind of future together, he didn't know. He'd ruined Cass's life.

He dragged his overnight bag from the cupboard and slammed it onto his hotel bed, giving the television a wry glance. It had done little to distract him from the turmoil he was in.

He flipped the bag open. At least she wasn't married to a slime like Sebastian. That much he could hang onto as a good thing that came out of the last disastrous hour.

The rest was a tragedy.

He didn't know what had possessed him to tell her his feelings for her. It wasn't the right time. He should have let her cool off, digest the disaster her wedding day had turned into, understand how he'd been caught between a hard rock and his sister. Now, there wouldn't be a right time for them at all.

Matt threw his shaving kit into the bag on the bed, casting a last look around the room for anything he might have left. Nothing. Nothing to keep him here for a second longer.

He picked up the suit-bag and strode to the door. He'd return to the ship and get back into work. Work was safe.

The doorman hailed him a taxi.

Matt couldn't believe he'd ruined a wedding and lost Cass all in one fell swoop. He could barely breathe at the thought.

He yanked open the door on the taxi. 'To the airport.' There was no point in sticking around. The hurt in Cass's eyes had said as much, if not more, than her harsh words.

Cass had made it abundantly clear where she stood. And that was nowhere near him!

Cassie ran into Sebastian at the altar. The reporters had gone so there was no head in hands, no slouched shoulders, and no watery eyes now.

She put her hands on her hips. 'Tell me where he's staying.'

Sebastian looked up at her. 'Who?'

'You know who. Matt Keegan.'

'Goodness, I have no idea.' He looked down at his shoes.

She bit down on her bottom lip. 'I could walk out that door straight into a reporter's welcoming questions. I'm sure I could tell him all sorts of things.' She dropped her eyes to his body. 'The sort of things that tabloids drool over.'

Sebastian stared at her. His Adam's apple bobbed up and down. She could see his imagination running wild. He pulled his belt up, and hooked his fingers in the leather. 'It's over, Cassandra. Let the poor man be.'

'Tell me, Sebastian.' She had no idea what Matt's

story was supposed to be to her but she could read Sebastian's pale face as though he were a cereal box. 'Because I have some last words to throw his way.'

He appeared relieved. 'I might have heard him say something about his hotel…'

'What hotel?'

'The Millennium. You *are* okay with all of this, aren't you? I know it's a blow and all, not marrying me, but—'

'Goodbye, Sebastian. I hope you receive in abundance all things coming to you.'

'Why, thank you, Cassandra.' He gave her his best smile.

She crossed her fingers and glanced at the beautiful stained-glass windows. She prayed Sebastian would get everything he deserved, and more.

Cassie gripped the front desk at the hotel. Her mind grappled with the concierge's words. Matt was gone. She took a deep breath. She couldn't lose him now. Not now. 'Who would know where he went?'

The concierge shrugged. 'Maybe the doorman knows.'

Cassie urged the taxi driver to go faster. She stared out the window and watched a jumbo jet take off. She took a deep breath, stilling the turmoil in her mind, in her body. Please let it not be too late.

She knew it was crazy to go racing around Sydney after Matt. She could just get an investigator to find him, but that could take weeks. Maybe he was even in the phone directory... But there was no time to waste. And the odds were, if he was anything like her, he'd go back to the ship and lose himself in work.

Cassie practically threw the money at the taxi driver and ran into the airport. The departure lounge for international flights was a mass of people.

Her heart pounded in her ears, her breath ragged. It seemed hopeless. Tears stung her eyes as she scanned the crowds, turning in a circle, her feet in one spot. The ache in her chest stretched up her throat as the hopelessness of the situation sank in. He'd probably already gone.

Cassie turned back towards the exit.

She froze. Matt sat stiffly in a chair with a newspaper. Her heart hammered. She took a deep calming breath and walked up to him. 'What time is it?'

His fingers gripped the paper a little tighter. He lowered the expanse of newsprint, his gaze careering slowly over her as if in disbelief.

'I'm not naked again, am I?' Cassie looked down at herself, offering him a small smile.

'Cass.' Matt's voice was strangled. 'What are you doing here?' He managed a smile, then sobered. 'You made it clear where you stand. I respect that. I'm leaving. You don't have to worry about seeing me again.'

She crossed her arms in front of her. 'That's why I'm here. I have a problem with that.'

'Really?'

'Yes. I want to see you.' She couldn't help but

smile. 'I want to see a lot more of you, in every sense of the word.'

Matt closed the paper and dropped it to the seat beside his. 'And why would you want that?'

She leant closer to him. The pressure in her chest was intense. This was it. She took a long deep breath. She had to take a chance on love. She looked into his gorgeous dark eyes and all her concerns melted at the deep love she saw there waiting for her. 'Because I want to give us a chance.'

'And why should I believe you?' he whispered.

She managed to laugh. 'Matt, I may know all the facts now, but I missed what was really important.'

'And what is that?' His tone was cautious.

'That *I love you*, Matt Keegan.' And just saying it, out loud to the man who made her feel so alive, warmed her entire body. She held her breath.

'Cass.' His reached out his hands to her.

She took them without hesitation. 'I love you,' she said again, floating in the pure ecstasy of being able to say it, and feel it, so deeply...

Matt drew her to him, coaxing her down onto his lap. He slipped a warm, soft hand around her neck and pulled her to him, kissing her with all the love she wanted.

'I thought I'd lost you,' he whispered finally.

'No. I just got too involved in the wrong things, with logic, with expectations, with the past.' Cassie squeezed him tightly. 'But I made it.'

'Yes, you did.' And he kissed her again, banishing all her fears.

*   *   *

Cassie and Matt burst through his hotel door in a flurry of arms and clothes, buttons and shoes, lips and hands. She couldn't get enough of him.

Matt kicked the door closed and froze.

Cassie turned. The television was on and the images on the screen seeped into her mind. It was *her* wedding. She saw herself going down the aisle.

'That's you.' Surprise was in his tone.

The images flashed to Eva and Sebastian in a clinch in the back room. They were celebrating their little victory very intimately.

'How do you suppose the media got that?' Cassie looked up at Matt, the smile on his face that of utter satisfaction. 'There were no cameras in that room.'

'Yes, there was mine. I mustn't have turned my camera off.'

Cassie smiled. Somebody must have found the video in the back room and passed it on to the press. She gnawed her lip. Sebastian's career was not going to fare well.

'Well, we've been splashed all over the news!' Cassie leant up against his hard body. 'I think I'd like to lie low for a while.' She smiled up into his dark eyes. 'With you.'

He wrapped her in his warm arms. 'Sounds good to me.'

'Everyone got exactly what they deserved.' She kissed his neck, teasing his flesh with her teeth.

Matt swung her off her feet and strode into the bedroom. 'Let me show you just how much you deserve.' And he kissed her, soundly, thoroughly, all over, and all night.

Much later, Cassie lay still, her head resting on Matt's chest, her heart full of love. She wasn't sure what the future would bring, but one thing that she'd learnt was that love was worth the risk.

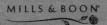

Become a Panel Member

If YOU are a regular United Kingdom buyer of Mills & Boon®
Modern Romance™ or Tender Romance™ you might like to tell us
your opinion of the books we publish to help us in publishing the
books *you* like. Mills & Boon have a Reader Panel of Modern and
Tender Romance readers. Each person on the panel receives a short
questionnaire (taking about five minutes to complete) every third
month asking for opinions of the past month's Modern and Tender
Romances. All people who send in their replies have a chance of
winning a FREE year's supply of Modern or Tender Romances.
If YOU would like to be considered for inclusion on the panel please
fill in and return the following survey. We can't guarantee that
everyone will be on the panel but first come will be first considered.

Where did you buy this novel?

❑   WH Smith
❑   Tesco
❑   Borders
❑   Sainsbury's
❑   Direct by mail
❑   Other (please state)

What themes do you enjoy most in the Mills & Boon® novels that
you read? (Choose all that apply.)

❑   Amnesia
❑   Family drama (including babies/young children)
❑   Hidden/Mistaken identity
❑   Historical setting
❑   Marriage of convenience
❑   Modern or Tender drama
❑   Mediterranean men
❑   Millionaire heroes
❑   Mock engagement or marriage
❑   Outback setting
❑   Revenge

- ❏ Sheikh heroes
- ❏ Secret baby
- ❏ Shared pasts
- ❏ Western
- ❏ Forced proximity
- ❏ Mistress heroines

On average, how many Mills & Boon® novels do you read every month? ————————————————

Please provide us with your name and address:

Name: ——————————————————————————
Address: ——————————————————————————
————————————————————————————————
————————————————————————————————
————————————————————————————————

What is your occupation?
(OPTIONAL)

——————————————————————————————————

In which of the following age groups do you belong?
(OPTIONAL)

- ❏ 18 to 24
- ❏ 25 to 34
- ❏ 35 to 49
- ❏ 50 to 64
- ❏ 65 or older

Thank you for your help!
Your feedback is important in helping us offer
quality products you value.

The Reader Service
Reader Panel Questionnaire
FREEPOST CN81
Croydon CR9 3WZ

FREE

2 BOOKS
AND A SURPRISE GIFT!

We would like to take this opportunity to thank you for reading this Mills & Boon® book by offering you the chance to take TWO more specially selected titles from the Tender Romance™ series absolutely FREE! We're also making this offer to introduce you to the benefits of the Reader Service™ —

★ FREE home delivery   ★ FREE gifts and competitions
★ FREE monthly Newsletter   ★ Exclusive Reader Service discount
★ Books available before they're in the shops

Accepting these FREE books and gift places you under no obligation to buy; you may cancel at any time, even after receiving your free shipment. Simply complete your details below and return the entire page to the address below. **You don't even need a stamp!**

YES! Please send me 2 free Tender Romance books and a surprise gift. I understand that unless you hear from me, I will receive 4 superb new titles every month for just £2.60 each, postage and packing free. I am under no obligation to purchase any books and may cancel my subscription at any time. The free books and gift will be mine to keep in any case.

N3ZEC

Ms/Mrs/Miss/Mr ....Initials ....
BLOCK CAPITALS PLEASE

Surname ....

Address ....

....

....Postcode ....

Send this whole page to:
UK: FREEPOST CN81, Croydon, CR9 3WZ
EIRE: PO Box 4546, Kilcock, County Kildare (stamp required)